SLOCUM WAS THE PRISONER
OF A SADISTIC COLONEL

He didn't stand a chance unless Ghislaine Marchand would help him, and now she was very efficiently digging his grave. Perhaps he should have responded to her open invitation on the train the night before. Had he done so, he was sure that his present situation would now be much more favorable. He shrugged. It was too late now. He had learned a little more about women, but it wasn't going to be of any practical use this time. He took a good look at her. She did look very tasty, he decided. It was going to be his last look at a woman, and at least she was beautiful. . . .

JAKE LOGAN

SLOCUM'S WOMAN

PLAYBOY PRESS
PAPERBACKS

I want to thank the following:
*Verrazano, Cornelius J. Kolff,
American Legion, Private Joseph F. Merrell,*
and *Gov. Herbert H. Lehman.*

SLOCUM'S WOMAN

Copyright © 1976 by Playboy

Published simultaneously in the United States and Canada by Playboy Press Paperbacks, New York, New York. Printed in the United States of America. Library of Congress Catalog Card Number: 76-9585.

Books are available at quantity discounts for promotional and industrial use. For further information, write to Premium Sales, Playboy Press Paperbacks, 747 Third Avenue, New York, New York 10017.

ISBN: 0-872-16745-3

First printing January 1977.
Fifth printing April 1980.

1

John Slocum was sitting in a saloon in Brownsville, Texas. He had spread out a copy of the *El Paso Weekly Tribune* on the saloon table. He was half-reading the paper, half-listening to the conversation that boiled around him. There were two stories in the paper that particularly interested him since he had quite a lot of money to invest.

This money was the result of what he liked to call "a forced donation" from the unwilling teller of the Cattleman's Bank of Denver two months ago.

The first story was concerned with the fact that the U.S. Government, having impounded 1100 horses and a similar number of rifles, was going to sell them at public auction next week in El Paso. They had been confiscated when a certain General Ortega had crossed the Rio Grande, fleeing from the troops of President Díaz. They would be sold, for cash or certified check, to the highest bidder in El Paso next Thursday at 10:00 A.M.

The second story described the recent uprising in the Anglo-Egyptian Sudan. England was struggling to raise and supply several cavalry regiments, and her resources were already considerably strained in India and elsewhere in Africa.

Slocum quickly deduced that the buyer of Ortega's impounded horses and arms would find a quick and lucrative market in England.

Even more interesting was the conversation around him. Slocum was overhearing none other than General Ortega himself, at the next table, sadly complaining, in Spanish, about the U.S. Government's confiscation and his new need for horses, rifles, and money. Slocum recognized the general as soon as he had entered the saloon by the photograph that the *Weekly Tribune* had run as an accompaniment to the story.

Slocum lit a cigar. He calmly began working out the intricate calculations his mind had to face now. He had money to invest. The government was selling all those horses and rifles. Most likely the Anglo-Egyptian Sudan could use them, not to mention General Ortega, who did not have any money. The cigar was a hand-rolled Havana. Slocum enjoyed it. It amused him to observe how the ash lengthened on the end without falling off. He tried to see if it would remain that way till he had smoked it down. The ash had built up to a fragile gray cylinder when it finally fell. As Slocum brushed the ash off the table onto the floor, he heard Ortega say in English, "Vairy good!"

Slocum looked up. Ortega was grinning at him and nodding at the cigar. Now he could take a good, careful look at the man and his companion.

Ortega was a thickset man with a husky voice. He had two gold teeth in his lower jaw. He had an alert, cautious, but not unpleasant, expression. He had big ears and black shaggy hair. The face of Arango, Ortega's companion, was flat, bronzed, and rugged. He was short, with strong, broad shoulders. From time to time, as he looked around the room, a curious glittering expression filled his brown eyes. Then they relaxed into a sleepy languor.

Slocum did not like him. In the middle of his right hand was a big scar, as if a .45 bullet had gone through. It did not seem to affect his use of the hand. Slocum noticed that the man's grip on his glass was firm.

Slocum stood and bowed. It was a good introduction and he decided to take immediate action. He had made his decision.

"Gentlemen," he said in the faint Southern accent he used normally, unless there was a need to disguise himself and his background, "might I buy the both of you a drink?"

Ortega's face showed polite curiosity. It was clear to Slocum that the man did not understand English. Arango, however, nodded with a smile. Slocum joined them. He offered the two Mexicans cigars from his battered pigskin case.

"Many thinks, *señor*," Arango said politely. "We like more cigarettes." They lit their harsh Mexican tobacco, the paper scented with licorice, and let the smoke slowly exude from their nostrils as they studied Slocum. They chatted for a while about the weather and the local women. Slocum knew Mexico and her customs well. He had once lifted a huge herd from Sonora and had quietly and expertly inserted it into Arizona. He did not, therefore, force the slow, courteous, languorous conversation.

He weighed the advantages of pretending not to know Spanish. On a short-term relationship they were manifold: People would say things they were sure he did not understand, and so forth. But if things went well, he would be involved with these two intelligent and tough men for months. It would be impossible to keep his excellent knowledge of Spanish a secret that long. Moreover, someone in Mexico who knew him might greet him in Spanish. Ortega and Arango would not like being deceived. And they did not look like the kind of men who would shrug Slocum's dereliction off.

They were impulsive and cruel. They would consider

him a traitor—and the life of a traitor below the border was stamped out as quickly as a scorpion's.

"I see that General Ortega does not speak English," Slocum said in Spanish. "If he wishes I will be happy to speak in Spanish."

"Good, good," said Ortega with a delighted smile. "But you speak our language well."

"*Sí*," Slocum said casually. "I have dealt many years in Mexican cattle."

"But you speak it much better than a *Tejano*!"

When Ortega said the word that meant "Texan," he pursed his lips with distaste as if he were biting into a sour lemon. Slocum knew well the hatred Mexicans had for Texans.

"I come from Mississippi, *señor*," he said.

"Mississippi?"

"Another state of the *Yanquis, mi general*," Arango said. He stared at Slocum with a thin, faintly skeptical smile. Slocum at that point knew that he and Arango would clash sooner or later. "Many *Tejanos* come from Mississippi, *mi general*," Arango added.

"*Verdad*," Slocum said. "But although I do much business in Texas, *no soy Tejano*." He knocked the ash off his cigar and contemplated Arango pleasantly and gravely, his face revealing nothing of the growing annoyance with Arango and all his ways.

"Are you afraid what will happen if we think you are a Texan?" Arango asked.

Ortega looked at Slocum with bright interest, as if his days of boredom in Brownsville were coming to an end. Slocum thought that the man had simple tastes. What Ortega liked more than anything else was to fight or to see a fight.

"You afraid?" Arango repeated. His eyes seemed to sparkle. A little smile curved his thin lips. Slocum looked at him with swelling anger. Slocum had had to kill

8

people, but he had had good reasons. He did not like to do so. But Arango, Slocum saw clearly, *liked* to kill people. Something would have to be done about the situation and quickly, before it got out of control. Slocum could keep his temper up to a point, but he knew he could not be responsible for his actions once that point had been reached.

Slocum slowly removed his cigar. A blur of movement followed so fast that neither Arango nor Ortega could have any clear image of Slocum's right arm. When it was over, Slocum was slightly bent over, his right hand under the table and pointing directly at Arango's stomach. It was done so quickly and so quietly that no one else in the saloon had even noticed.

"No," Slocum said. *"Y usted?"*

Ortega burst into delighted laughter. He slapped the palm of his hand flat on the table in enjoyment. Arango's gun hand was nowhere near his weapon. He dared not risk going for it. His face paled. Slocum knew that it had not whitened in fear but in a cold rage. He did not move because he knew it would not profit him at all; his rage existed because he had made a wrong estimate about Slocum's behavior.

"Listen, Luis," Ortega chuckled, "he said *usted* and not *tu!*" The distinction between the polite and the familiar forms of the word *you* was important in Mexican social intercourse, and the joke implicit in the usage of the polite form by someone holding a gun was, for Ortega, an uproarious witticism. "He's a real *caballero*. He's no *Tejano! Señor—señor——"* He paused with an inquiring look.

"Mitchell."

"Sí. Señor Mitchell. My friend Luis made a joke. And you made a better one. And now, let us be friends."

"Cago en—" Arango began to mutter an insulting Mexican curse.

"We are in the United States, *cabrón!* Shake hands!"

Slocum understood the implication of those two sentences. It was not that North Americans shook hands to make up. It was simply that in Mexico, Arango or Ortega could kill anyone they wanted and that would be the end of it. In the United States there were unpleasant legal technicalities, sometimes ending with a running noose at the end of a *reata* and a slap on the flank of a horse patiently standing under a tree or a telegraph pole.

"But——"

"Shake hands, *burro!*"

Arango grudgingly extended a hard brown palm. Slocum brought his right hand up from under the table. In it was his cigar and nothing else. Arango's face reddened. Ortega burst out into wild, convulsive whoops of uncontrollable laughter until everyone in the saloon turned around to stare at him. He finally subsided.

"Oh, my God," he gasped. "Jesus, Maria, and all the saints! Oh, my God, how funny!"

Arango's palm was cool—his shake was not firm and friendly. This did not surprise Slocum. What did surprise Slocum was that Arango's palm was dry. Almost any other man's hand in that situation would be dripping with nervous sweat.

Slocum knew that Arango would never forgive him for that little act of humiliation. He shrugged. Some risks were worth taking, in order to teach people to keep civil tongues in their heads. But it looked like Arango was incapable of learning.

Slocum reinserted the cigar in his mouth and said, "Gentlemen, I have a proposition."

"Ah?" said Ortega, intrigued.

2

"First of all," Slocum said, "I know who you are."

Arango shrugged with contempt. "So?" he said. "That knowledge is had by everyone in Brownsville." He pronounced the word *Browns-villy*.

"Yes. I also know your problem."

"*Sí*," Ortega said. "Money. So?"

"Yes. You need money. Money buys horses, rifles, ammunition, food. Once you have horses and rifles, the men will come."

"Yes!" Ortega said, showing excitement. "And with an army we will overthrow the son of a whore down in Mexico City and bring freedom to Mexico!"

Slocum did not believe the latter part of that sentence. But he did not want to say so. Slocum was not in the least bit interested in whether or not Mexico was a dictatorship under the old dictator, Díaz; all Slocum cared about was whether or not the country was a fertile area for his contemplated investment.

"*Sí, mi general*. Now, I see that the government here is going to sell your horses and rifles at a public auction in a few days up at El Paso."

"*Sí*. On Monday. Bastards."

Arango laughed. Slocum did not like the sound. Ortega looked at him impatiently. He turned back to Slocum and asked what his plans were.

"Very simple. I will go to El Paso, bid on the horses and rifles, and get them."

"The government here is not stupid," Arango retorted. "If they suspect that you will sell them to us, they will not sell to you."

"True," Ortega said. "Your government gets along very well with Díaz."

11

"It is all a waste of time," Arango said. "Then someone else might outbid you. It is all hot air."

"Everything is possible," Slocum said calmly. "But let us understand two things. One, you need horses and rifles—which you can get with money. Two, I have money. Therefore, I might be able to use my money to make all three of us happy. With your permission."

"I—" Arango began, but Ortega cut him off with a sharp command to shut up. Arango subsided.

Slocum continued. "Now," he said, "no cattleman I know down here—or anywhere—can use all those horses all at once. And since your horses were not of the best— and since no one can use all of those rifles, which were probably badly maintained as well—the government will not look at me too closely. Particularly when I tell them I have already lined up a sale to England, and that England needs rifles and anything on four legs for her troops in the Sudan—and quickly. She can't afford to be too demanding at this point."

"It is a good story," Ortega said thoughtfully. Arango shrugged.

"Then I will buy the horses and rifles. Whatever price I buy them at, I will then sell them to you as follows: Seventy-five dollars for a horse, forty dollars for a rifle."

"But you might get the horses for as low as twenty, twenty-five dollars!" Arango said.

"Shut up, Luis!" Ortega said. "*Señor* Mitchell is entitled to a profit."

"But he is selling us *our* own horses!"

"May I point out," said Slocum genially, enjoying Arango's rage, "that they are *not* your rifles and horses? They are the property of the *Estados Unidos del Norte*. They were *once* your property—although I have the feeling that your title is, as lawyers say, somewhat cloudy —but it will be only with my initiative and money that they will become yours once more."

12

"True, true," Ortega muttered without heat. "And you will buy them? How?"

"With cash. That will give me immediate title. Then I will move them immediately before Díaz hears of it and tries to stop me."

"Cash?" asked Arango thoughtfully.

Slocum knew clearly what the man was thinking. Arango was thinking it would be a good idea to kill Slocum, take the money, and line up some American to bid on the horses and rifles. The American would give the auctioneer the same story that he had thought up.

Slocum discouraged this little dream of Arango's.

"Cash, sure," said Slocum easily. "I'll pick it up at the bank, just before the auction, and I'll hire a couple of good men as bodyguards."

"Ah?" asked Arango casually.

"Sure. I never know if some son of a bitch might pick up my word. Besides, I'll need some men to handle the horses on the train till I can deliver. I have some old friends in El Paso I can call on for help."

"*Y entonces?* And then?" demanded Ortega.

"Then my men will load the horses. We will stock two extra boxcars with enough oats to feed them to New Orleans—where, as far as the government is concerned, they will be going to wait for the next ship to Alexandria. But—the train will stop at a siding east of El Paso."

"Very good," said Ortega approvingly. "*Pero un momento.* But wait a moment. Why are you so good to me? I am not a person whom *gringos*—with your permission—like. Why then?"

"I want to invest money in Mexico," Slocum said truthfully. "My 35,000 dollars will get me nowhere with Díaz, who is used to dealing in millions with big bankers, big railroad men. But if I help you now —when you need it badly—and if you win—I expect to be paid back."

13

"Yes. You will get your investment back."

"With interest," Arango said with his hard, tight smile. Slocum did not like the implications of that remark. He chose to disregard it.

"I can get better interest in my bank in El Paso, *mi general*, where conditions are somewhat more stable. No. If you win, you will remember that I helped you when you were without a *centavo*. It is a big risk. True?"

"True," Ortega nodded.

"*Bien*. I want a big interest."

"How much?"

"The railroad concession for Chihuahua and Sonora."

"But you don't know anything about building railroads!" Arango said angrily.

"No. But I will sell the concession—and there will be my profit."

"Too much!"

Slocum said simply, "Big risk. Big interest."

"And if I say no?" asked Ortega.

"Then, *señors*, let me buy you a drink and wish you the best of luck in your glorious enterprise. I will look for another investment."

Ortega lit another of his licorice-flavored cigarettes and blew the smoke at the dirty ceiling. "How do you know—after I take Mexico City from that coyote—how do you know that I'll keep my promise?"

"Because," said Slocum, "you will give me your word of honor as a Mexican general."

Ortega was flattered. That meant nothing much toward keeping his promise, as Slocum well knew, but it was something. It could be mentioned in critical times —and there were bound to be critical times, as Slocum was well aware. Critical times were what Mexico specialized in.

It was not the kind of an investment that a careful man would enter upon. But careful men passed their

14

lives in a mental country that was flat and without scenery. People who took chances had mountains in their lives. And valleys, too.

"*Momento*," said Arango. He took Ortega by the arm, leaned over, and whispered.

"*Con su permiso*," Ortega said politely. The two men stood up and moved to the end of the bar. Arango spoke briefly and with heat. Ortega nodded thoughtfully. They returned to the table and sat down. Ortega motioned to Arango to speak. He began without preliminaries.

"How do we know that you are not an agent of Díaz? We go into Mexico with the horses and there he will be waiting for us. Common sense, no?"

Slocum had not expected this.

"It is possible, is it not?" asked Ortega courteously. Slocum noticed that the man's eyes were hard.

"Possible."

Ortega's eyes narrowed in his hard evaluation of Slocum's face. Slocum took a long pull on his cigar and exhaled slowly, watching the smoke rise and eddy. Ortega's stare unwillingly followed his.

"You are too calm, *señor*," Arango said.

"Ah," said Slocum lazily. "And if I were furious, you would then automatically believe my denial? You are childish, *amigo mío*."

Arango's face flushed. He started to get up, but Ortega, without looking at him, placed a hand on his shoulder and forced him down into the chair once again. By the smacking sound that Arango's rear made in its sudden contact with the chair seat, Slocum could tell that Ortega was a man of great strength.

"He is right, Luis," Ortega said.

"If you suspect my motives—and you have survived this long precisely *because* you are suspicious—" here Slocum bowed courteously to Arango, who grunted a reluctant assent—"all you have to do is the following.

15

When the train with the horses leaves El Paso, you will place your men anywhere you want along the tracks. You will have three hundred miles to pick from. You will cut the telegraph wire early that night, so there will be no way for anyone to send messages. You will signal—we will agree upon a signal—and when the engineer sees the signal he will stop the train. Your men will be waiting."

"What about ammunition?" Arango growled.

"I will take care of that."

"Easily said," Arango muttered.

"And easily done. Money weighs heavily on everyone's scales."

"*Si, si,*" nodded Ortega.

"But the ammunition is of several dimensions," Arango said stubbornly. "It is not reasonable that the government of England would ask you to ship such ammunition on a long voyage. It would deteriorate in the salt air. Especially when they have such ammunition themselves."

"But I was not thinking of *buying* ammunition," Slocum said. He enjoyed their puzzled expressions for a moment.

"You are making a joke?" Ortega said. His expression showed he did not think kindly of this.

"No. There is ammunition in Mexico of all these calibers?"

"For those with money, yes."

"*Bien.* If I am successful in my bidding, I will give you two thousand dollars in gold. You will buy ammunition, and when the rifles come into Mexico, you will be ready."

Ortega's eyes widened.

"And then," Slocum went on, "you will bring the horses into Mexico with the rifles; ammunition will be ready. You will be in Mexico, at any place you choose, with Díaz completely unaware of your entry point. And

16

when he finds out—and he will, soon enough—he will hesitate to attack a thousand well-armed horsemen."

"True, true," Ortega said slowly. He turned to Arango, who shrugged. *"Nada más?"* Ortega demanded. "Nothing more?"

Arango shrugged again. Good, Slocum thought. The bastard has run out of ideas. But not permanently. Bastards do not run out of ideas permanently. He will produce others. Slocum looked at the man's heavy-lidded, impassive face. Arango had placed his right palm on the table, extended and closed his fingers, and kept repeating the gesture, as if his hand were an accordion. It was probably to exercise the muscles of the hand, somewhat damaged because of the old bullet wound. But the movement became irritating to Slocum after a few moments.

"Good!" said Ortega decisively. He reached across the table and shook hands with Slocum. Arango followed suit, but reluctantly.

"But I make one condition," Ortega said. "When you build your first railroad, you will give me and Luis a lifetime pass. Agreed?"

"Seguro."

"No pass for me, *mi general,*" Arango said.

"Why not, *cabrón?*"

"I don't need a pass. I'll just get on and the conductor will know who I am. He'll be afraid to ask for money."

"On our friend's railroad," Ortega said, "you will behave like a gentleman and not like a *burro* from the mountains, do you understand?"

"I don't want a pass. Cowards use passes. I——"

"Listen, *maricón!* You——"

"Señors! Please don't fight. You have been inactive too long. Soon you will get all the fighting you can handle."

"Bien," Ortega said, relaxing. "I want to get out of

17

this goddamn *gringo* country and go to Mexico. I'm going crazy sitting here without money."

"*Señors*. A suggestion."

"*Sí.*"

"One of you will come with me to El Paso. General Ortega will take my two thousand dollars and go to Mexico. There you will get your men ready to receive the horses and rifles when they come off the train. The men's pockets will be full of the ammunition you will buy in Mexico. They will have saddles and bridles. You will keep in touch with one another. How you do it is not my concern."

"*Sí*. And then?"

"When I put the horses on the train, *Capitán* Arango will pass the word to General Ortega. And you, General, will signal the train at night, anywhere east of El Paso you like."

The two men stared at him, fascinated.

"Go on."

"Two lanterns, both going up and down. Clear. Cannot be mistaken for any brakeman's signal. The engineer will be bribed. He will have his instructions. He will stop the train. Your men will be waiting. In ten minutes the horses will be off. I will have crowbars. In a few minutes more, the crates will be opened. In half an hour you will have an army ready for a campaign."

"*Ay, caramba!*" shouted Ortega, heedless of the startled glances from the other tables. He turned to Arango. "*Muchacho!*" he said, "I'll make this *gringo* a colonel! The first good horse I take will be sent to him! What intelligence!" Arango sat in silence beside Ortega, flushing dull red from jealous anger.

"Eh. Luis? A man like this *gringo*? He can plan battles!"

"*Sin duda*," muttered Arango. "Without doubt."

Slocum smiled to himself. The curt two words of praise had been extracted from Arango like a back molar. Slocum was very careful to conceal his amusement. Arango did not like him as it was. There was no reason to add to that mass of resentment. It was already simmering like lava.

"I'll leave right away, Luis," Ortega said. "You know how to reach me."

"*Sí, mi general.*"

Ortega turned to Slocum. "In a week, then, *señor*," he said. Slocum nodded. He had left 3000 dollars with the bartender for safety. He went up and asked for 2000 dollars. The man produced them in the form of gold double eagles from the safe. Slocum counted them out into a buckskin bag and handed it to Ortega.

Ortega took the bag, smiled, and held out his right hand. Slocum extended his. "I trust you, *señor*," Ortega said. "Do you trust me?"

"Evidently," Slocum said dryly.

"Good," Ortega said. "Let us see who is stronger." He squeezed as hard as he could, but Slocum had done hardrock mining; he had worked hard at roundups; he had dug ditches for irrigation in hard-packed clay soils. His back and shoulders were covered with a hard muscular sheath, and his palms, from checking bawling calves, were as tough as leather. Ortega squeezed even harder. Slocum decided, for diplomatic reasons, that it would be best to let Ortega win. He squeezed back, then winced and yielded.

"You are, *mi general*," Slocum said regretfully.

"*Hasta luego*," Ortega said, grinning in triumph. "So long. See you in a week."

Yes. In a week, Slocum thought. In a week both of you bastards will resume your killing of anyone who disagrees with you. But that's where the money is. He knew that once the deal was consummated, he would have to sleep lightly and be very, very careful. *That* was the way to stay alive in Mexico—and also the way to get out of there with money.

3

Slocum arrived in El Paso the day before the auction. He took a room at the Long Branch Hotel with a bathtub. Bathtubs were still very scarce west of Denver, but the alternative was to step out in the back yard and dump buckets of water over himself. That had its advantages, but then where could he leave his money belts?

Therefore, he took the room with the bathtub, paying double the usual rent. He groaned with pleasure when the weight of the gold coins was removed from the criss-crossed money belts on his shoulders. The skin was beginning to chafe badly, like a horse with a poorly arranged saddle blanket. He had had the belts made to order. There were two wide straps over his shoulders, supporting the four rows of little pockets; each pocket had a flap and a small button. Each pocket held three or four coins.

He climbed into the tub, soaked, scrubbed, toweled himself. He put on the belts again with a muttered curse, donned clean underwear and dressed. He left his laundry at the desk and went out scouting for four bodyguards to attend him at the auction the next day, and also to help handle the horses on the train.

He found four out-of-work cowboys who were delighted to make 20 dollars each for a couple of hours' work the next morning. They agreed to meet him at the Rio Grande Valley Bank the next morning at 9:00. Next, he went to John Sisson's Saddlery and bought a small satchel. He then went to the Rio Grande Valley Bank and opened an account. He deposited 20 gold double eagles. He waited for his bankbook, which was made out in the name of Theodore Mitchell. He smiled to himself as he thought of the perfectly legal withdrawal he would be making the next day instead of the usual kind, which was usually carried out to the sound of shots and a few carefully chosen threats.

He ate a quiet dinner in a decent restaurant near the hotel. It had a clean red-and-white checked tablecloth. He savored the fried chicken, corn on the cob, cornbread, stewed tomatoes, and most tantalizing of all, the tall glass of fresh cold milk. Slocum knew that he would not only not see that particular kind of food for some time, but he was also sure he would not see a red-and-white checked tablecloth south of the border, let alone a clean one.

Satisfied with the meal, he left the Chinese waiter a good tip. He walked slowly back to his hotel, enjoying the coolness of the evening after the day of blistering valley heat. He climbed to his room, jammed a chair under the doorknob, took off his shirt, and took off the heavy weight of his money belts. He groaned silently with pleasure as the weight slid off his shoulders. He rubbed the shoulders, shoved the Colt under his pillow, blew out the kerosene lamp, and gradually fell asleep.

4

Slocum was outside the bank next morning at 9:00 with his new satchel under his arm. It was full of gold coins, which he had removed from his money belts and placed inside the satchel before leaving his room. He carried the satchel so that it looked empty. He stood in front of the plate-glass window, over which the words RIO GRANDE VALLEY BANK were curved in an elaborate gold-leaf Spencerian script, with intricate arabesques

21

spiraling off the R, the G, the V, and the B. He yawned. To casual observers, such as the Mexicans who seemed to be idly sprawled across the street, Slocum must have seemed sleepy and completely unaware of his surroundings.

In five minutes the four cowpunchers he had hired as bodyguards the day before ambled up. They were all armed with the heavy Frontier Colt model. The Mexicans across the street knew that the men and the guns were not there by accident.

"Mornin', boys," he said. "I'll be right outside."

As the men settled down to wait, Slocum looked into the bank window at the reflection therein of the four Mexicans across the street. The tallest one, a thin brown man with a scraggly mustache and the huge sombrero of the North, was talking to the others. They had clustered around him, and as he spoke he was staring at the four bodyguards, unaware that Slocum could see his every movement reflected in the glass. Slocum saw the man point a finger and thumb, pantomiming a gun. The Mexican then pulled an imaginary trigger. The four men rose and stood there in deep thought for a moment, watching Slocum carefully.

A little idea of Arango's, Slocum realized. He entered the bank. He wrote out a check and handed it with his bankbook to the teller, who had been looking nervously at the four cowpunchers as they loitered outside, leaning against the window, and occasionally looking in.

"My bodyguards," Slocum said, quieting the man's fears. He handed his slip to the teller.

"All?"

"All. In silver dollars, please."

The teller counted out 400 silver dollars. Slocum scooped them up in both hands and dumped them on top of the gold coins already there. The satchel now had a satisfying bulk and heft to it. To any casual examiner, it would seem that there could be all of 35,000 dollars in it.

When he walked outside, the four cowpunchers fell into step behind him. Slocum suddenly cut across the dusty street and stopped in front of the Mexicans. Their faces immediately froze into impassivity.

"*Buenos días,*" he said amiably.

"*Buenos días.*"

"My respects to your friend."

"My friend?" the man said, with a good attempt at portraying bewilderment. "I do not understand, *señor.*"

Slocum shifted the heavy satchel to his other hand. The heavy clinking noises riveted the Mexicans' attention. Slocum was pleased.

"Well, then," said Slocum genially, "if you don't know who I'm talking about, then there are no messages to give."

He opened the satchel. The man's eyes widened at the sight of so many silver and gold coins. He reached inside and pulled out four silver dollars. He held one out to each man. They held out their palms, pleased yet bewildered.

"It's thirsty work, waiting," Slocum said and strode off to the auction. Scraggly Mustache smiled reluctantly.

5

The auction was held in the lobby of the Cattleman's Hotel. Grimy wicker chairs were scattered about on the dusty carpet, with badly polished brass spittoons strategically placed. But only two other bidders showed up. One of them represented a glue factory in Galveston and dropped out when the bidding went over ten dollars, while the other bidder, who owned a firm that bought up cheap rifles to trade to native African elephant-ivory poachers, refused to go over 12 dollars each for the rifles. So Slocum took the horses for 12 dollars each and the rifles for 15. This meant that he had paid out 29,000 dollars for the material at the auction; he had given 2,000 dollars in gold to Ortega for ammunition. This left him a total of 4,000 dollars for expenses and escape money. But if he should walk out of Mexico with that railroad concession, he would be worth millions.

"Do you have a certified check, mister?" asked the auctioneer.

"Cash."

He opened his satchel and counted out the money. He paid the bodyguards and thanked them, pointing out that they could make a little more money if they'd help him take the horses to New Orleans. They were willing.

"Well, sir, when will you take possession?" asked the auctioneer.

"Soon's I line up a train."

"An' the rifles? They're crated over at Fort Bliss." Fort Bliss was a few miles outside of El Paso.

"Same."

"Let me have your name, sir. And home address. I'll notify the fort commander right away that you are now the legal owner. He'll release them."

Slocum gave him his new name and a hotel address in Denver, where he had once stayed under that very name for a one-month period. In the last five years Slocum had used eight names for various interesting enterprises. It was lucky for him that he had a good memory and could remember which name he used where.

The glue man, a fat fellow with a shabby Prince Albert frock coat stained with countless memories of gravy-saturated meals, asked, "Where d'ye plan to take your horses?"

Slocum raised his eyebrows and said nothing.

24

"Not that it's important, mister," the man added hastily.

"It's not important," Slocum said. He took his receipt, carefully folded it, and placed it in his wallet. He turned to the glue man. "Don't mind tellin' you, sir," he said, "they're goin' to be shipped out to Egypt."

"Sure! They got a war goin' on down there, ain't they?"

"Yes."

"Say, mister, that's pretty smart!" The man looked enviously at Slocum. With the man's loose mouth, Slocum had no doubt that the information would be all over El Paso by nightfall. He would then go to Fort Bliss, where the citizens would have a deep interest in where the horses would be going. The information would serve to relax the commanding general.

Slocum stepped out into the blinding glare of the border sun. It was only a two-block walk to the stockyards where the horses were held. The horses weren't much to look at. Most of them were sturdy little mustangs, and they could survive on whatever grass they could crop on those desolate plateaus. They ate leaves or even the green inner bark of cottonwood trees. Slocum had once had a Mexican horse on the Gulf Coast that would eat fish when nothing better was offered. The mustangs would do fine in a desert campaign once they were back under Ortega's men.

He went into the stationmaster's office. There he spoke to the yardmaster and arranged for 33 cars, one to contain the crated rifles and enough oats for the trip to New Orleans. He paid in advance. What Slocum particularly liked was that little touch of paying for the trip all the way to New Orleans when the horses would not even go a tenth of the distance. Things like that distinguished Slocum's ventures: imaginative little additions that made

25

people feel relaxed and completely trusting. He never tried to cut corners with expenses. He told the yardmaster he'd have ten men ready when the train pulled out of the yards to handle the horses on the way to the port of embarkation for Egypt.

"They c'n keep their bedrolls in the car with the grain and rifles," the yardmaster said, "seein' that you'll be guardin' the crates anyways."

"Damn right!" Slocum said with heat. "Some of those Mex generals would sure like 'em. This train goin' to be an express?"

"Hell, no, mister. It ain't no fruit train. It'll leave after the passenger train goes through. Don't forget, it's gotta make several stops so's your men c'n carry water for your stock. We don't want it interferin' with important traffic."

Good. There'd be no train following to get nosy about another stopped train ahead in the middle of the desert. He told the yardmaster that his ten men would be boarding the train that evening. The signal to the engineer would be two lanterns moving up and down.

"Can't you pick up any men in El Paso?" the man demanded. "I c'n get you plenty who could use the work."

"Sure you could. But I want men who know how to handle horses. I don't want any swampers out of saloons who need some money while they sleep off their hangovers. My consignee will only take horses in A-1 condition. I want *my* men, an' they'll be gettin' on tonight maybe fifty, sixty miles east of here."

"It's mighty irregular, Mr. Mitchell."

"That's right," Slocum retorted with the annoyance of an independent entrepreneur who had just invested a lot of money. "Do you think I *want* my horses unfed and unwatered? I've already wired my ramrod to have 'em ready."

26

The yardmaster shrugged. "I s'pose you know what you're doin', Mr. Mitchell."

"Damn right!"

The yardmaster opened the bottom drawer of his roll-top and pulled it out. "Some firewater?" he asked.

"Why, you bet."

The man would have some tough explaining to do next morning to the division superintendent. In a sense, Slocum thought regretfully, it really wasn't fair for the yardmaster to present his own liquor to the man who would be causing him grievous problems. But that was the kind of thing Slocum often found irresistible. As a way of expiating his sin, he told several dirty jokes to the yardmaster, who laughed uproariously. Slocum was willing for the man to extract some pleasure out of this relationship. He shook hands with him, hired a hack outside the yard, and rode out to Fort Bliss. There he arranged for the delivery of the crated rifles to the yard. He did not worry about Ortega receiving notification that the deal had been consummated with the army of the United States. Obviously there were people, such as Scraggly Mustache, who would keep the general well posted about everything.

Late that afternoon the train was made up in the yard. Then it chugged slowly to the holding pens. The side doors were opened, straw was spread on the floor, and the horses were driven in up the loading chutes. Slocum made sure that they had a good feed of oats and their fill of water first, since, of course, there would be no cowpunchers on board to handle them during their several hours on the train.

All that Slocum knew was that sometime during the night, the horses would leave the train. The grain and water would have to last till then. The train finally pulled out a little after 7:00. Slocum rode in the caboose with the conductor and the brakeman. There was a Winchester carbine in a rack just above and to the left of the door. He noticed that neither of the two men in the caboose with him carried a gun. When the engineer stopped for water at a tower 24 miles east of El Paso, Slocum stood up, removed the cartridges from the carbine, and replaced it on the rack, before the two men returned. Slocum thought that the conductor, a hard-bitten little man of 50 who said little, would show fight in the crisis to soon develop; it never hurt to take out a little insurance. Slocum only shot when it became absolutely necessary.

The engine whistled several times in a staccato burst. "That's for me," said the conductor. "That's probably the lanterns up ahead." He poured out the coffee, kept at a low simmer on the stove.

"I'll have some of that coffee first, thank you kindly," Slocum said.

It would be his last cup of American coffee for a long time. He gulped it down. He had discarded his wealthy rancher's outfit back in the hotel. He now wore the traditional cowpuncher's outfit: strong Levi's, a flannel shirt, plain leather boots without any elaborate stitching, and short businesslike spurs. He wore a Colt in his gun belt. The car with the crated rifles carried his saddle, saddle blanket, slicker, and bedroll, as well as a pair of saddle bags with his changes of underwear and socks, shaving gear, and odds and ends. The train jerked to a full stop. Slocum swung down the steps and walked toward the two lanterns and the dark figures clustered around them.

6

The engineer leaned out of his cab, staring at the men standing beside the tracks. When he saw Slocum walking up from the caboose, he shook his head in disgust.

"Now, look, Mr. Mitchell, these damn men of yours, I didn't know they was greasers. Not a goddamn one of 'em understands English. I been tellin' 'em to get inside the second car an' they keep lookin' at me!"

Slocum nodded. There was a half moon, which gave good light. The two lanterns had been set down between the two rails on the rock ballast, and standing in back of the lanterns was Arango.

"*Muy buenas noches*," Slocum said.

"Let us not waste time," Arango said curtly. This was not good manners, and Slocum did not like it. "I would like to kill the train crew immediately," Arango went on. "Then we won't have to waste time talking."

"I see no need for that."

"Come on, come on!" yelled the engineer. "I ain't got all night! Stop that goddamn Mex yappin'!"

"I would like very much to kill him," Arango said. "*Ahora mismo!* Right now!"

"There is no necessity, *mi capitán*," Slocum said politely, detesting the man. "One moment."

He turned and climbed into the cab. "What the hell's goin' on?" demanded the engineer.

In Slocum's back pocket were several piggin strings made from rawhide. He took them out now with his left hand while with his right he pulled his Colt.

"What the Sam Hill!" began the startled engineer.

"Better let me do it," said Slocum. "If they do it, they're likely to get absentminded and kill you. Turn

29

around. You too, fireman!" They put up their hands. Slocum tied up the two men.

He climbed down and told Arango to start unloading. He added that he would take care of the conductor and brakeman. He walked down the length of the train to the caboose, where he had spent the last hour chatting with the two men. As he began to climb up the little ladder, the conductor flung open the door, pointed the Winchester—which had occupied a little rack beside the door —at Slocum's heart and pulled the trigger. Slocum didn't move, but thanked God for his thoughtfulness for carefully removing all the cartridges at the last water tower when he had been left alone in the caboose. He tied up the conductor. The brakeman had fled into the darkness, but several of Arango's men easily caught him and returned him in good condition. Slocum tied him up, too, and put him next to the conductor.

By now the rifles were off the train, and the crates had been ripped open with the crowbar Slocum had brought along. Slocum climbed the nearest telegraph pole and ripped the wire down. He climbed down, twisted the loose wire around the cowcatcher, unhitched the locomotive, and, releasing the brake and pulling out the throttle, steamed ahead slowly.

"You a railroad man?" asked the engineer, watching Slocum's moves with professional interest. Slocum did not believe in casual conversation. He said nothing. One by one, as the locomotive proceeded, the taut wire snapped off its insulators, twanging in huge loops for a distance of 300 yards. Slocum stopped the locomotive.

"You shore look like you know how to handle this yere ol' steam dog," said the engineer admiringly. Slocum recognized the danger of giving out autobiographical information to a witness. Again he did not respond. But once, down on his luck, he had been a fireman on the

Northern Pacific. The engineers up there had taught him enough.

Slocum jumped off. He told one of the men to wrap the telegraph wire a couple round turns around his saddle horn and gallop a couple miles into the desert and leave it there. The repair crew would never find it, and they probably wouldn't come equipped with the extra wire necessary to fill the gap. Thus the news of the disappearance of the shipment would be delayed a few hours more.

The sliding doors had been opened. Ramps had been set up, and the horses were being led down. From the bushes came saddles, saddle blankets, bridles, and bits. Occasional cries of joy burst out as some lucky man recognized his old mount. The night was filled with the clatter of hooves as the horses went down the wooden ramps, shrill neighs as the horses trembled with excitement and the pleasure of being released from their cramped quarters. To this was added the metallic jingle of the bits, and the creaking as hundreds of saddles were flung over the saddle blankets, adjusted, and cinched tightly, with murmured endearments and curses as the stubborn ones resisted and plunged.

Once in a while someone, whose pockets were full of the caliber of the cartridges that fitted his rifle, could not contain his publicly announced happiness over that fact. He would celebrate by firing several rounds into the air. It was getting to be a typical Mexican *fiesta*, Slocum saw, and the fact that it took place at night in the desert beside a railroad did not worry anyone. Nowhere did Slocum notice Ortega or Arango.

After an hour everyone had a rifle that more or less pleased him; the same was true of the horses. Later on, both rifles and horses would be traded around amongst themselves, till some sort of an equilibrium would result.

31

More horses would undoubtedly show up in the looting, which would be the inevitable accompaniment of this peasant army's march into Mexico.

Well, so what? That was not Slocum's problem. *His* problem was to cover his bet, and the only way to do that was to cross the Rio Grande with what were legally his horses and rifles. But his suit for payment was not legally enforceable in any jurisdiction in either the United States or in Mexico. The ultimate judge in the case of John Slocum, plaintiff, versus General Rafael Ortega, defendant, was holding court on Slocum's right hip. His name, of course, was Samuel Colt.

7

Slocum had suggested to Ortega that each man bring three *sisal morrals*. All the *morrals* were now filled with the oats from the supply on the train. Thus, his men would be able to move quickly across country for the first critical three or four days without spending valuable time on foraging for the sparse grass—a problem that President Díaz and his federal troops did not have to face. Since the federal armies could use plenty of quartermaster depots and the railroads, they could make swift movements with their St. Cyr–trained officers. They were formidable opponents and would have to be treated with great and respectful caution.

So it was lucky for Ortega that Slocum had foreseen the foraging problem and had so neatly solved it. It had not occurred to Ortega. Slocum hoped that Ortega would remember and be grateful; however, Slocum had learned that people in power had neither gratitude nor long memories for favors done. Slocum would have no hesitation in reminding Ortega.

By sunrise Ortega's army was organized across the Rio

Grande, safe from United States internment—that is, organized as well as it would ever be. It was an unpaid volunteer army. Its soldiers had drifted away when the corn was ripe, or when the fields had been planted, or the hillsides burned to make fertilizer for the new crop, or when calves had been branded. Such work was too hard for the women to handle. Campaigns had to be planned so as not to interfere with these important matters. It was lucky for Ortega that the corn had been planted recently. The women and young boys could handle the chores around the fields and pastures.

Slocum had marked out a fine sorrel for himself. While throwing a saddle blanket over its back, he pondered over the incident that took place between the conductor and himself. Although the conductor's Winchester was better than his, he did not take it. He had been so shaken by the trigger being snapped at him that he had lost control for a few seconds. He had grabbed it by the muzzle and had smashed the stock and the trigger mechanism over one of the rails. It had shaken him more than he cared to admit. Only his instinctive ability to foresee certain events had saved him this time.

The rebel band rode northwest through the chilly, cloudy night, their leather saddles creaking through the tiny villages. At San Pedro de la Sierra, a little after midnight, he met Ortega. Ortega and Arango had dismounted and were squatting outside a little hut with a thatched roof, munching on *tortillas* and eating roast chicken.

"*Oye, gringo!*" Arango called out, waving a chicken leg. "You did a good job across the river! Sit down and eat."

Not until the invitation had Slocum realized how hungry he was. He had not eaten since noon of the day before; he had been so charged with excitement that he had forgotten to eat.

33

He accepted a plate of chicken from the silent Indian woman who was cooking inside the hut. He ate hungrily. Ortega looked at him in a friendly manner; Arango stared in his usual half-insolent, half-impassive way, which made his moves hard for Slocum to figure out in advance. Slocum munched his food, deciding he could always count on Arango doing the unexpected—and whatever that turned out to be, it would not be for Slocum's good.

Ortega suddenly stood up, tossing the clean chicken bones to the scrawny mongrel dogs, prowling around out of kick-range. They fell upon the bones with hysterical snarls. Ortega wiped his face on the back of his already filthy, greasy sleeve. As far as he could see, little fires burned as his men cooked the chickens and turkeys they had bought or stolen in the night's march.

"*Hombre*," he said proudly, turning to Slocum with a sweep of his greasy fingers, "I've got an army again!"

He sat down and began on another chicken leg. "But," he went on, "this army is making too many enemies. We have to steal from the peasants in order to live. No good. Very bad. We need *Don* Porfirio to feed us. So we do two things first. We ride to Juárez. There is a big military train due there early tomorrow morning with a big son of a whore general in command. We take the train. Luis will run it. He is very good at running trains. You will see. Then we take the bank in Juárez. That will give us money, much money! We get maybe fifty, a hundred men killed. No good, but we need the money in the bank. With the money we pay the men. Now they will pay for their *tortillas*, their chicken, their whores. They don't have to rape anymore. Now the people will like us! Then we put the horses on the train and go south. Then we catch that son of a whore pimp fairy Díaz and we hang his balls in the bell tower of the Cathedral in Mexico City. I will become president of Mexico, Luis will be the general of all the armies, and you, *amigo mío*, shall have your railroads!" He beamed.

"And my 35,000 dollars?"

"*Seguro que sí*! Absolutely!"

"When we take the bank."

"*Sí, Claro.*"

"Suppose we need the money to pay the men?" asked Arango.

There was danger here, Slocum knew. He would have to move carefully here. A tactical retreat was a good idea.

"Only if the money can be spared, of course," said Slocum.

Arango spread his hands sidewards, palms up, and shrugged.

"Of course," he said.

"Then we have no problems," Slocum said pleasantly. Something told Slocum that, if they did take the bank successfully, Arango would be telling him, regretfully, of course, that the bank had very little money.

It might, therefore, be a good idea to be on hand at the looting of the bank. Just to protect his interests. He was somewhat of an expert in these matters. On the other hand, it would be dangerous. He might be shot, either by the bank guards, or, regretfully and accidentally, of course, by Arango or one of Arango's men—who could be later instantaneously shot as an expression of Arango's apology, should Slocum only be slightly wounded.

Slocum would have to play it by ear.

8

"The best time to attack," said Arango, "will be just before sunrise. They'll be sleeping and a little drunk." Ortega grinned as he listened. Arango had told him that he wanted to plan this operation, and since he had never done so before, Ortega was willing to listen.

It was almost noon. They were standing on a *chaparral*-covered ridge two miles west of the railroad. Juárez lay five miles to the north. They could make out little square green patches showing inside the gray adobe buildings. These were the *patios*. Everything else showed up a dusty gray and brown. The army depot, with its quartermaster supplies, was a massive square building one mile south of the town. A railroad spur led to it from the main line of the Mexican Central. The tracks ran right into the depot, and a huge wooden gate made of oak barred any access into the army depot unless the gate was opened.

Gray dust powdered the trees and bushes around the three men. Arango had removed his huge *sombrero* and was swinging it gently back and forth, the edge of it just missing his dusty boots. Ortega sat cross-legged next to him, listening to his plan. Occasionally he lifted up a pair of field glasses that he had confiscated from an unwilling landowner only three days before. He scanned the railroad tracks to the south. Then he rested the glasses on his knees, cursing softly.

"The train is late," he said.

Slocum was sitting with his back against a small cottonwood tree, his long legs stretched out in front of him, idly tapping a small twig on the dry soil.

"The trains of Mexico," he said, "are on time. But only once every twenty-four hours."

Arango stopped swinging his *sombrero*. His voice was very soft and without emotion.

"*Momento, señor*," he said. "A little moment. Your statements do not in any way reflect on Mexico?"

"On the contrary," said Slocum pleasantly.

"Very well."

Arango resumed the slow oscillation of his *sombrero*,

36

as he resumed his discussion of tactics. He had a sheath inside his right boot. Now he reached down and pulled out his knife. On the back edge of the blade were etched the words *Who makes me come out will regret it*. Now he placed the point on the ground and made a map as he outlined his ideas.

"Gomez will take his men along the ravine here, that one which comes out of the tracks a mile north."

Slocum knew who Gomez was. He was the man with the scraggly mustache, who had spied on him in El Paso. There was a definite intelligence and reliability about Gomez that Slocum liked. Gomez was half-Yaqui, mostly given to silence. He preferred to ride barefoot. This embarrassed Ortega, who made him put on his boots whenever they rode through a village.

"Then Gomez will go around to the north of the depot, this way. Arias will go to the south, this way." Arango scratched another line with his knife. "I will start two hours before they do, circle around, and be ready on the east side of the depot. We will leave the west side open. We make a lot of noise. They will see how many we are, and they will get scared. They will come out and try to escape to the west, where they will not see anyone. But you will wait for them in ambush. *Bam bam! Adiós, Federales!*"

"Then what?" asked Slocum, not even looking up from his idle scribbling on the ground with his broken twig.

"Then what?" repeated Arango irritated. "I will tell you what. What is I am not interested in talking to you. *Claro?*"

Slocum looked up at Arango and his knife. He was thinking that the plan was terrible, and that the only way to get anything good out of Arango would be to shoot him and make jerky out of the corpse.

"Luis, *mi amigo*," Ortega said gently, "please. Our

friend said something which interests me. Then what? I ask that too."

"Then we kill them all, and we take the depot. We take what we want, we take the bank, we take the train, and we come south! *No hay problemas.*"

"No problems?" asked Slocum.

"No. No problems!" Arango said curtly.

"*Señor* Mitchell," Ortega said, "I think you see problems. I would like to hear your opinion."

Arango drove his knife three inches deep into the hard-packed soil with one swift, vicious stab. This took strength, and it was clear to Slocum that Arango wished to do the same to him.

"*Jesús y María y todos los santos!*" he said between clenched teeth. "Do you permit this *gringo* pawnbroker to discuss tactics?"

"Why not?" asked Ortega lazily, amused by Arango's anger. "The sea refuses no river. *Señor?*"

Slocum sat for a moment, thinking. His arms were folded as he stared down into the valley, which was shimmering in the heat. During the Civil War he had commanded a cavalry company. He didn't intend to mention that. The less anyone knew of his background the better. He still had a sister living in Mississippi. He had long ago decided that the less she knew about his activities the better. She had given him up for dead, and it was better that way, considering some of the things he had done since he had crossed the Missouri. But Slocum had his code: No cold-blooded murder for profit; no rape; no shooting anyone in the back. And no stealing from anyone who could not easily absorb the loss.

The sea refuses no river. He liked that. It was well said. Ortega had a bit of poetry in him.

"First of all," Slocum began, "who knows the country around Juárez and the depot like the back of his hand? You? Gomez? Arias? You, *mi general?*"

38

"No," Ortega said. "None of us grew up here or worked here.

"So," Slocum went on, "you have planned four separate movements. Each movement is to be made in the dark, in strange country, and they are scheduled to come together exactly at sunrise?"

"*Sí*," said Arango, in a surly mumble.

"It will not happen. Such movements are the most difficult in war, even with trained cavalry."

"You are wrong!"

Slocum never repeated himself. He shrugged and continued to scribble in the dust with his twig. Arango's arm suddenly slashed. His knife cut the twig in two. Slocum's hand instinctively dropped to his gun butt, but Ortega stepped between them.

"Luis!" he said warningly. "He is right. Remember what happened at Durango! *Señor* Mitchell, you seem to have a plan. What is it?"

Ortega's swift action and his calm, soothing tone had dampened Slocum's sudden rage. He was grateful. It would have meant the end of his investment and probably of himself on that isolated ridge had he shot at Arango.

"*Mi general.* I suggest that we forget all complicated maneuvers."

He was aware of Arango's stare. He noticed for the first time that the man's eyes resembled that of a pig— bold, demanding, closed to any appeal of any kind whatsoever. An old Mexican had once told Slocum that people with pig eyes should always be carefully watched and never, *never* trusted.

It would have been wiser, perhaps, for Slocum to keep out of these matters entirely, and thus avoid any clash with Arango. On the other hand, Slocum's wish to protect his investment carried heavy weight with him. He had decided, therefore, to concentrate on the second factor, and, at the same time, refrain, as much as possible, from exciting Arango. This would mean that he would have to walk a tightrope as long as he was in Mexico—but Slocum had a very good sense of balance, except when one of his uncontrollable rages swept over him in a tidal wave of fury. He could resist one of those attacks no more than a bather could resist a real tidal wave suddenly sweeping in from the ocean depths.

It would be all right as long as he did not get too mad.

9

The two men were watching him. "There's the train," he said, pointing. Far to the south they saw it, crawling busily along. A cow started to amble across the track. The train did not slow down. The impact booted the heavy animal several feet into the air. At that distance it resembled a tiny brown fly. It lay on its back as the train steamed on. Slocum had noticed that Arango's face had taken on an expression of excited delight. Slocum recognized that look; whenever he saw it in any of the men who had worked with him in any of his operations, he made sure to get rid of them.

Arango was now under control. He turned and looked at Slocum with his heavy, malevolent stare, and Ortega looked at Slocum with his usual calm and alert expression.

At the bottom of the hill on which they were standing stood a water tank. Slocum stood up now and stared at it, thinking hard. Behind it, due to the constant, slow seepage of water, grew a huge grove of cottonwoods.

"Our *gringo* Napoleon is thinking," Arango said with heavy sarcasm. Slocum paid no visible attention to the remark.

It was normal for military trains to carry a flatcar

40

with sandbags piled along the edges. The chances were good that this train would have such a flatcar. Slocum borrowed Ortega's field glasses and verified his hunch. There was also a pullman, much more ornate than the usual grimy, unwashed car in service on Mexican railroads. Probably it was for the officers. Most likely it was a private car that had been sent down from the States, and which then had been coolly seized by some high officer for his own use, and to hell with the legal problems.

Soldiers were sprawled lazily behind the sandbags, ready for an attack.

"All right," Slocum said decisively. "Send five of your best shots to the water tower down there. When the train stops for water, let the men pick off the soldiers on the flatcar. You will also have a troop waiting inside the cottonwoods. Make sure they are out of sight. They will cut off the engineer and the fireman from getting back into the cab. Others will ride along the train, ready to take care of any resistance. All done in daylight. No one will get lost; no complicated time schedule to follow."

"*Bueno, bueno!*" exulted Ortega. He stood up.

"It looks too easy," muttered Arango.

"There is more," Slocum said, paying no attention to Arango's remark. "We will then fill the train with our men. We go nicely to the spur leading to the depot. I know how to work the switch points. Then, once on the spur, we go at full speed. Right through the gate. Everyone inside will think the engineer is drunk. They will run out, yelling; they won't be carrying weapons. When they are all outside the barracks, we will open fire. We will take what we want, back out, coal up, throw out what we don't want, put on the horses, go to Juárez, take the bank, and go south again on the train, with transportation, supplies, and money."

"But——" Arango began.

41

"No time for 'buts'!" Ortega said sharply. He rapped out orders. In less than five minutes, horses were being spurred down the hill toward the green mass of the cottonwood grove.

10

Slocum's feelings were correct: The train hissed to a stop at the water tower. The engineer and fireman climbed down, swung the water pipe into position, stretched their arms lazily, and ambled casually around the engine. A few soldiers peeked sleepily above their sandbag barrier. They had stretched canvas sheeting over the tops of the sandbags for some protection against the harsh Chihuahua sun. Seeing the water tower, they grabbed their canteens, jumped down from their flatcar, and strolled over to the tower. All of them left their rifles behind. Slocum counted ten cars; probably not more than thirty men in the flatcar, and perhaps, he guessed, fifty or so men scattered through the rest of the train.

Arango was in the cottonwood grove; Slocum was secretly hoping that the son of a bitch would get himself killed in this little action, but it was beginning to look as if it wouldn't happen today.

Nothing was happening down there. It became clear that Arango was letting the crew fill up the tank before he attacked.

"*Mira!*" Ortega chuckled, passing the binoculars over to Slocum. "Look! Luis doesn't want to do the work himself later. I know him, Wait, as soon as they finish, he will attack. You will see."

Sure enough, as soon as the fireman swung the filler pipe away, the firing started. Slocum smiled. Arango had his points. Ortega clapped his back in glee. The startled soldiers sprinted for their flatcar and their rifles, but those men who were not shot in the first three volleys were ridden down by the sudden charge of the horsemen from the shelter of the cottonwoods. None of them managed to reach the flatcar.

Several men dismounted, climbed to the roof of the train, and then ran along the top of the cars, shooting off their rifles in exuberance. The engineer and fireman were backed against their locomotive with their hands in the air.

"Let's go down," Ortega said. "Your plan was a good one!" When they reached the railroad, Arango was busily looting the dead. Ortega rode on beside them, completely oblivious. He chatted happily with Slocum. Not a single one of his men had even been wounded. Nineteen federal soldiers had been killed, their naked bodies sprawled grotesquely beside the train.

As they came alongside, Arango rode up with a grin. He held a Colt in his right hand.

"Very good, Luis," Ortega said approvingly.

"*Sí*. Wait till you see what we found, *mi general!*"

He turned and rode back. As he passed each body he fired downwards. Ortega paid no attention. Evidently, Slocum observed, he was used to this behavior on Arango's part. Each bullet entered the skull. It was pretty good shooting for a man on horseback. Slocum filed this information carefully away in his memory. Slocum never forgot anything like that. That was how he had managed to survive in the West ever since he had left his ruined home in Mississippi years before.

Arango dismounted and waited impatiently for Ortega and Slocum to do the same. He went up the stairs of the ornately decorated pullman, which Slocum had first noticed 20 minutes ago through the binoculars. When they had climbed after him, he entered the vestibule, turned, grinned, and crooked a finger. They followed him, consumed with curiosity at what Arango had found that had caused such delight.

11

Inside the pullman car, a thick red carpet lay on the vestibule floor. Arango put a dirty hand on the ornately carved brass doorknob on the stained-glass door, opened it, and called out with mock courtesy, "I take great pleasure in presenting General Ortega!"

The thick blue satin curtains covering the windows had been drawn against the fierce desert light. It took several seconds before Slocum's eyes adjusted to the dim light.

What he had first taken for a mass of white pillows piled on one end of a long, red velvet covered couch was not pillows, but a beautiful woman, clad in a long white muslin gown. She had long black hair caught up in several circular coils, each one piled on top of the one below it. She had pale, clear skin with eyes the color of the deep blue Arizona sky. She was tall. Her legs were crossed at the knee, and one small foot, encased in a white silk-topped shoe, was swinging angrily back and forth. Each white arm was flung broadside along the back of the couch.

Opposite her, on the other side of the pullman, sat a man on a carved oak chair. He wore the blue uniform of an officer in the army. His tall, thin figure was topped with a pepper-and-salt cropped military pompadour. His thin mustache was neatly trimmed. He was staring at the carpeted floor. He was clearly not enjoying the situation.

"A general!" Arango boasted. "Not bad, eh?"

Ortega nodded, beaming. He clearly enjoyed the

contrast of the general's uniformed splendor against the grubbiness of his own troops, what with their floppy *sombreros* and crisscrossed *bandoliers*.

"I give her to you, *mi general*," Arango said, with a wide, careless sweep of his right hand. Slocum noticed that Arango's ring finger had suddenly sprouted a wide gold ring with three large diamonds embedded in it. Arango noticed Slocum's glance at the ring and added, grinning, "A little present from the general." The general's face did not change expression.

"What's your name?" Ortega demanded bluntly.

"General Arturo Romero Cisneros," the man said quietly but with distaste. "I demand to be treated as a general. I demand that my ring be returned, which this animal took from me. And I demand that *Señorita* Ghislaine Marchand be treated as a lady and not as an Indian woman."

"Why?" Ortega asked lazily. "What did he do that does not appeal to you, *mi general?*"

"He put his dirty paws inside my dress," the woman said with a cold fury. Slocum recognized the faint trace of a French accent.

Ortega smiled. Arango's smile was even wider.

"And I also demand——" Cisneros began stiffly, but Arango interrupted him.

"*You* demand nothing, *gachupin!*" grated Arango. Cisneros knew he was very close to dying. He flushed at the old insult toward anyone of Spanish birth, but he was sensible enough to fall silent.

"A suggestion," Slocum said. It was time to put a stop to this explosive situation: Arango liked to kill people, and Slocum did not want to see any more of that behavior if he could prevent it. It was clear that Ortega had very little objection to this propensity on the part of Arango.

"*Sí?*" Ortega said.

Slocum had already observed that Ortega was always ready to drop anything he was doing or thinking in order to listen to Slocum's suggestions. He had found that they were usually practical and simple and cost very little in lives.

"Let us take the bank *now*. Before we take the depot."

"Why?" Ortega was intrigued. Arango, too, like a child with a sudden new toy dangled in front of him, had temporarily dismissed his quarrel with Cisneros. Perhaps, thought Slocum, he would drop the whole thing if he could be drawn even further into some new tactics.

"If we take the depot now, word will reach town before we get there. The banks will lock their vaults and will be armed and waiting for us, and the vaults, even if we do get inside the bank, will be impossible to open."

Arango shook his head, grinning. Ortega nodded at him. "He knows how to persuade people to open vaults."

"But suppose the man dies under your persuasion? Suppose he gets killed as we take the bank?"

"Possible," said Ortega thoughtfully.

"Let us leave the horses here," Slocum went on. "We take the train into town. You dress in the general's uniform. *Capitán* Arango and I will be sergeants. We dress up thirty of our men as soldiers. We are very annoyed with them. We march to the bank. They are recruits. They are stupid. We yell at them. You hit them with the flat of your saber, you are so enraged at their clumsiness."

"Go on!" Ortega loved it. Arango was fascinated, although he made every effort to hide it.

"We stop in front of the bank. The recruits come to the at-ease position. You, *mi general*, will enter the bank. You demand to talk to the president of the bank. We two sergeants and a squad follow. The rest of the men stay outside. They will take care of any police who may

46

become too interested. The president comes out of his office—or does not; it does not matter. When the time is ripe, we enter the vaults. We tie up everybody, if it is necessary. Or we can leave a receipt. It will say this is a forced loan to *Don* Porfirio. What can they do? It has happened before. We march back to the train. Everyone will think it is by *Don* Porfirio's orders. We go to the depot. They certainly will not expect us. We take the depot. We back the train to the main line, we go south, pick up the horses, *y adelante!*"

"*Ay, caramba!*" breathed Ortega. "*Que valiente! Seremos una leyenda por todo México!* What guts! We shall be a legend all over Mexico!" Arango's eyes were shining.

"*Sí,*" Slocum said gravely. Arango had forgotten his recent passionate wish to kill Cisneros. Besides, the plan might just work because of its insane boldness.

Slocum turned to Cisneros and waited. Cisneros smiled in reluctant admiration and began to unbutton his tunic. The woman looked at Slocum with a cool, approving stare. Slocum understood that look; it meant that one meal-ticket had been found to be unserviceable, but that another one was on the horizon. As the general undressed, he caught the look. A rueful expression appeared on his face. Catching Slocum's eye he gave a tiny shrug, as if to say, what would one expect of a whore?

Ortega had sent out a soldier to bring back two sergeants' uniforms. They arrived, dusty, wrinkled, and soggy with blood surrounding the bullet holes. He tossed the uniforms on the couch beside the woman.

"*Mujer!* Clean these up and sew the holes. Neatly."

She did not move. A faint flush appeared on her cheeks. Ortega moved till he stood over her.

"You heard?"

She stared straight ahead, as if he did not exist.

47

"I think you had better do it, my dear," Cisneros said.

She turned angrily to face him, but he held up a hand and said wearily, "It is a very little thing to do in order to live."

He had great dignity, even if clad only in his underwear.

She tried to speak again, but once more he held up a hand and said, "You are a prisoner. These men are animals."

"*Animals?*" said Ortega. "*Gachupin* son of a whore, a Díaz officer raped my mother! Animals?"

"*Mi general?*" said Arango, with a question in his voice.

"Go ahead," Ortega responded. Before Slocum could move, Arango put three bullets into Cisneros's stomach, and when the shock of the heavy .45-caliber slugs had forced Cisneros to bend forward, Arango placed two more in the man's chest at a distance of three feet. The sound of the blast in that confined space was agonizing. She turned white and bit her lower lip till a drop of blood appeared, but she did not scream. There was no sound. The air was filled with the acrid, pungent stink of gunpowder. Cisneros slid to his knees, choked once, and died.

Arango *was* an animal, Slocum thought. But this was neither the time nor place to mention it. Arango knocked out the empty cartridge casings, filled the cylinders and slid his gun back into the holster. His eyes had lost that glittering shine that had preceded the shooting.

"Throw out the garbage," Ortega crisply ordered.

One man took Cisneros's shoulders, another the feet. Ortega opened the door of the car to the vestibule. A cluster of curious men stood outside on the roadbed. They moved aside as the body was casually tossed into the bushes. Arango went through the pullman, pulling out drawers, dumping out their contents, paying no attention to Cisneros's blood, which he calmly walked through as if the floor of the car was a muddy swamp necessary to cross.

Slocum watched Arango's rummaging. "You do that very well, *mi capitán*," he said, with mock admiration. "You have had lots of practice."

Arango was not insulted. He laughed and continued his searching. Finally, in a small wicker suitcase, he found what he was looking for: a small sewing kit. He tossed it onto the woman's lap. Ortega nodded in pleasure.

"Get to work," he said curtly.

12

The bank job went off perfectly. The bank personnel, convinced that the general was either insane or obeying the orders of *Don* Porfirio, made no resistance. No one was shot. However, there had been some big withdrawals by various mining firms in the last few days, so that all they managed to scrape together in the bank's own canvas bags was 47,000 pesos, most of it in silver.

A few people noticed the neatly repaired knife and bullet rips in the fabric. They saw no point in mentioning this. The phony recruits looked extremely awkward as the commands were bawled out in front of the bank, and many passersby stopped to smile. No one was hurt. Ortega was pleased.

The train steamed southward from Juárez. Ghislaine remained in the pullman, under guard, pacing restlessly back and forth. The freight cars were jammed with armed men, delighted at receiving money for the first time in months. When they reached the spur leading eastward to the depot, Slocum made the switch and climbed back into the cab. He had thrown away his uniform and was dressed in his usual work clothes. Arango had killed the engineer because he liked to run locomotives himself. It was as simple as that. He had kept the fireman alive because he didn't want the bother of training someone for what was a job of some skill.

Slocum had suggested it might be better to wait outside the gate to the depot. No one would suspect the train had been seized. The bodies had all been flung over horses and then dumped into a distant *barranca*. The telegraph line to Juárez had been cut. Patrols sent out by Ortega made sure that no one had approached the depot.

Arango disagreed with Slocum's suggestion. It had become immediately clear to Slocum that Arango was like a child, longing for the excitement of driving a locomotive through a locked gate. Every engagement for Arango had to have all the excitement of the Fourth of July. Otherwise where was the fun in being a soldier? But Arango, Slocum noticed, disagreed calmly. It seemed that his emotional equilibrium was always in balance after he had killed a few people.

Ortega backed Arango. The three men were in the cab of the locomotive. Several rifles lay on the floor of the cab, ready for action, and each man, now in the traditional rancher's outfit of northern Mexico, wore the crisscrossed *bandoliers* filled with rifle cartridges. The locomotive rounded a curve. Two miles ahead lay the square depot, with guardhouses at each corner. Horses grazed idly by the track, and they could see tiny figures moving in and out of the door that had been cut into the bottom of the big gate. A small box to one side of the gate was obviously the sentry post. Everything dozed or moved slowly in the hot sun. Children, playing inside cactus hedges enclosing the front yards of shanties, waved up at the cab. Arango waved back with a wide grin.

"Andale!" shouted Ortega. He liked the excitement of the romantic approach just as much as Arango—who now shoved the throttle to full forward. The train began to gather speed. Arango leaned out of the cab, a wild grin splitting his brown, usually sullen face. Ortega turned to the white-faced fireman, who knew what they were planning to do.

"More coal, *hombre*, more coal!" he shouted.

The man worked desperately, scraping his big coal shovel into the coal tender, and then twisting the shovel so that it sprayed fresh coal evenly over the red-hot mass inside the furnace. Even Slocum felt the excitement and grew jubilant as the steam pressure built up and the big driver wheels spun faster and faster.

When the train was half a mile away, the waving people beside the tracks realized that the train was moving too fast. They stared in astonishment and yelled at Arango, urging him to slow down. Slocum looked at Arango. Arango may have known how to handle the controls of a locomotive, but it was becoming clear to Slocum that the man knew very little about mass and dynamic inertia—that is, the tendency of an object in motion to remain in motion. A train of 15 cars built up tremendous dynamic inertia, and Slocum would like the train to stay on the rails and not go through the buffer, which was, no doubt, placed at the end of track inside the depot. Too fast, and the train would continue on through the buffer and then for some distance inside the depot. Nothing would get it back on the tracks again except a wrecker unit, and he did not intend to hang around for that to appear, accompanied as it would be by some very vengeful federal officers. The train would have to be braked somewhere short of the gates in such a way that it would go through the gate all right, but stop somewhere short of the end of the track.

The wind was blowing Arango's hair wildly. He was

singing. The fireman's hands were visibly shaking as he slung the coal deep into the furnace. The locomotive was swaying and rocking, and the back blast, whenever the fireman opened the furnace door, was so intense that Slocum involuntarily held his hand up in front of his face. By now Arango was slapping the side of the cab and jumping up and down in his seat. Dogs, goats, and children seemed to be frozen in astonishment as the train rattled and banged ahead.

It was time.

Slocum jerked out Arango's Colt, leaned past him, pulled the throttle all the way back, let it go, and then pulled the brake to its last notch. Arango's furious, startled face swung to face him. His right hand had automatically dropped down to his holster, but, realizing his gun was gone, he knew he could do nothing, especially as the wheels locked and an ear-splitting squeal leaped up from the rails as the two metal surfaces exercised friction against the wheels. The entire train slowly began to lose speed. Slocum blocked Arango's movements toward the brake. In the midst of the horrible, high-pitched squealing from the friction of the locked driver wheels, Slocum could see, from the corners of his eyes, the startled faces of the guards as they fled from the sentry post. A fraction of a second later the 30-foot-tall oak doors shattered open in a screaming explosive spray of flying beams, iron bolts, and massive hinges. They were inside.

13

Afterwards, Slocum would admit that there was humor in it. Chickens squawked and fled; some piglets crossing the track moved faster than Slocum had ever thought pigs could move; soldiers stood with open mouths in the middle of their shaving at a long table set under a tree in the inner courtyard; and one woman dropped her laundry basket, fell to her knees, and began to pray frantically after her lightning performance of crossing herself. The locomotive hit the bumper at the far end of the courtyard. The only damage to the locomotive was that the cowcatcher had crumpled up like an accordion. Slocum's assumption of command had saved the train.

Slocum handed Arango back his Colt. "*Mas tarde, amigo*," he said and jumped off the train. Arango followed. Slocum had no doubt that he would, in fact, be seeing Arango later. The fireman lay flat on his stomach, trembling.

An officer had rushed out of his room. His suspenders were hanging down and he was incoherent with rage.

"You crazy son of a bitch!" he yelled at Arango. "You goddamn *cabrón*! You——"

Arango put a bullet in the man heart. All the doors on the freight cars opened. Hundreds of rifles stuck out. Slocum thought that the whole train looked like a long, gigantic pincushion. None of the federal soldiers in the yard were armed. A few ran for the barracks as soon as they saw the rifles, but they were shot down. Ortega's men leaped down from the cars and in a few minutes they had seized the depot, with its 120 men and eight officers, at a cost of one man killed and seven wounded—none seriously, mostly with the knives that all the soldiers carried on them.

The storeroom held several tons of corn. This served to fill up one end of a freight car. One storeroom held more than 100 crates of new lever-action Mausers, still in their original grease. The powder magazine produced more than 100 boxes of new Mauser ammunition. Ortega was delirious with joy as he watched his men filing into the storeroom and exchanging their old

53

ragtag weapons for the beautiful new rifles and filling their pockets with ammunition. Many of the men rushed outside as soon as they had wiped off the grease, and loading, fired exultant shots into the air. It was a stupid waste of what might serve to be irreplaceable ammunition, as Slocum knew, but he also knew that Ortega had to accept it. It was a traditional part of Mexican life. If you had a firecracker, you exploded it. If you had a skyrocket, you lit its fuse and screamed with joy as it went up. If you had a gun, you fired it, no matter how expensive cartridges were.

It went on for ten minutes. Then it stopped suddenly. Slocum hoped the cessation of the racket meant that Arango was finally acquiring some command intelligence.

Several hundred cases of canned meats were loaded on. Crates of boots went on, as well as shirts, pants, and underwear. Boots were being tried on and exchanged; blankets were being stripped from the soldiers' cots. While the cars were being loaded, Slocum strolled over to Ghislaine's pullman to see how she was getting on. After all, she was probably not used to violence, and she must have been getting her fill of it the last few hours. Two grinning sentries watched his approach. They had taken to calling him "General Gringo," after his impersonation in Juárez, and when he placed his foot on the first step, they barred his way. "Sorry, General Gringo. General Ortega is resting."

Slocum understood. The woman, after all, understood her position, and she was obviously smart enough to handle herself intelligently. After all, she was French, and had not been traveling with her federal General Cisneros as a tourist. Nevertheless, he felt a stab of jealousy. She did look far more intelligent than the usual girl in a cow-town crib. And far more attractive. He sighed and turned away.

Far away, at the locomotive, he heard Arango yelling,

"*Oye, gringo,* let's go!" Arango was leaning out of the cab, beckoning him over. Slocum walked the ten-car length of the train. All the men had been rounded up and put on the train. They had broken into the officers' liquor supply. Many of them were drunk and retching out of the sliding doors onto the courtyard into the mess already created by the splintered gates. Nevertheless, when they saw Slocum striding by, they grinned happily. One called out, "*Vive el general del norte!*"

Slocum grinned. He liked good-humored teasing. He climbed into the cab. Arango smiled at him. He was a little drunk, but under good physical control of himself. He was in the happiest mood Slocum had ever seen him.

"I'm going to drive this whore train all the whorish way to that big whore of a town, all by myself!"

"What whore town?"

"General Ortega and I, we talked about it just now, before he went back to test that French whore. There are some plans we do without talking about it first with that great general from Texas, *amigo mío. Comprende?*"

"I comprehend. Which town?"

"Torreón, *chico.* Torreón!"

Torreón, Slocum knew, was an important rail junction, and it also held a big federal garrison. Slocum did not think a few hundred untrained troops could take the city. But this was not the time for him to express any objections.

"*Sí, hombre!* We have plenty men, plenty rifles, plenty ammunition, plenty food!"

Slocum did not see where they were going to put the horses. He mentioned this politely.

"My friend," Arango said with exuberance, "don't worry!"

He flexed his right hand several times as if it pained him. Had he hit someone during the battle for the depot? Slocum did not notice any bruises on the

55

knuckles. Arango released the brake, put the locomotive into reverse gear, and inched the throttle forward. The train slowly began to move backwards. It would be doing so till it reached the switch on the main line. Then it would face south, its destination, Torreón, another 400 miles. The locomotive slid past the wreckage of the gates. Now Slocum could see the entire federal force piled in grotesque heaps along the outer walls. Each man had been shot once in the back of the head. He spun and looked at Arango, who now held up his right forefinger, crooked it as if it were curled around a trigger, and then resumed massaging his hand.

Slocum finally understood. What he had taken for the usual aimless firing into the air to celebrate a victory were the sounds of Arango's gun meticulously killing each man, one after the other.

For the first time the thought came to Slocum: I may have bitten off more than I can chew. It was a disheartening thought. He had been willing to play the game called "I'm the Only Gringo in Town," but this was different. A whole lot different.

14

The ten-car train chugged south. The strategy finally decided upon was to leave the horses back near Juárez in a little wooded valley. To take a big city like Torreón, argued Ortega, horses would be unnecessary. Particularly since space on the train would be minimal and if horses were taken along, then men would have to be left behind. And horses, Ortega pointed out, were not as good at shooting as men were. Moreover, too many stops would have to be made to water, feed, and exercise them. These added delays would give too much time for *Don* Porfirio to reinforce Torreón.

No. The troops, once in Torreón, would act as infantry. Once he had taken Torreón, Ortega said, he would hold it as a base. He would hold the rich Spaniards of Torreón as hostages, prying money from them whenever he needed any. Their other function would be to prevent Díaz from attacking, lest the well-known passion of Arango for shooting prisoners be given free rein. If he needed horses to campaign, he could easily confiscate them from the great *haciendas* that filled the huge ranch country surrounding Torreón. He made it all sound so simple and logical.

Slocum thought that Ortega was becoming over-confident, the usual reaction after too many easy victories.

"*Mi general*," Slocum suggested, "why not seize another train and use it just to transport the horses?"

Ortega made a valid objection. He said in order to do that he would have to wait three or four days until a train came along. It would probably be too well defended, since Díaz knew Ortega was active again. Therefore, to take any train would result in heavy losses. Better to move first, hoping to reach Torreón before Díaz could bring reinforcements from Mexico City. Slocum nodded. The chances were good.

The three men were sprawled out in the express car. Ortega was idly going through the mail, which he had found in 12 sacks destined for Juárez and the United States. If he found no money, he scaled the envelopes out through the open door into the countryside as it flowed by. They had spread some of the confiscated blankets over the full coffee sacks they had found in the car; the train's cat purred sleepily away atop one of the sacks. Arango had at first objected to the cat sleeping on top of the coffee, but Ortega insisted it was a clean cat. The rest of the car was a litter of saddles, bridles, and ammunition *bandoliers*. Two cots had been set up, one for Arango and one for Slocum, but the two men had discovered that blankets on top of the coffee sacks were more comfortable.

It was late at night. Arango had discovered that one of his men had once worked as an engineer on the Tehuantepec Railroad and had told him to take the throttle, cheerfully threatening to personally execute him if he made any mistakes. They both understood that the remark was not to be taken as lighthearted joking.

The sliding door was wide open. Two kerosene lanterns hung from hooks screwed into the ceiling planks, swinging wildly as the train creaked and rattled over the uneven roadbed. Ortega liked to look out of open doors. He said that the windows of the pullman were too hard to keep clean. Moreover, he added, "how could any man talk to any woman more than five minutes without being drowned in a flood of small talk about clothes, hairdos, dances, and furniture? There was only one thing a man should spend time with a woman for, and after that was over, he should leave as quickly as possible."

"I hope the lady is well," Slocum said politely.

Arango snapped his head upwards and stared at him.

Oh, yes, Slocum thought, the man *did* have pig eyes; he had seen such eyes in famished pigs watching their slops as it was being dumped into their feeding troughs. It was clear to Slocum that Arango considered it possible that the American's casual question might be used to exploit Ortega's sexual jealousy. And if it worked, there would be an end to Slocum.

"The lady is well," Ortega responded. "But tired." He grinned proudly. "I left her playing solitaire with a pack of playing cards, all made of *ivory*! And round as a ten-*peso* piece. She said a count gave them to her."

Ortega beamed with pride that he now had a mistress who had once actually belonged to a count, and who possessed such a marvelous thing as a deck of round ivory cards. There was something boyish and even charming about Ortega, Slocum decided, and he found himself liking the man, much to his surprise.

"Would you like to see the cards?" Ortega suddenly asked. "And also have a drink? Cisneros had some very good brandy. He had taste in brandy as well as women. I am enjoying both!" He raised his head to the sky and said ironically, *"Muchas gracias, mi general!"* Arango thought the remark was blasphemous, and crossed himself hurriedly, with a disapproving look at Ortega. But he said nothing.

They walked through the swaying train. The moon was full. Some men were sitting on the roof, dangling their legs over the side. Some were strumming the guitars that all Mexicans seemed to take with them wherever they went. Sometimes Slocum thought the guitars were as essential a part of their baggage as their rifles. A few men were singing to the sound of the guitars. Slocum loved the music of Mexico and the high, pure tenors whose songs ranged from sad, unrequited love to the most obscene and clever descriptions of Díaz and his generals. The smell of scorched meat and chili peppers hung in the air, rising from the fires being made in the cars below in boxes filled with sand. The moon was so bright that one could read a paper by it.

"Ah! *La luna mexicana!*" exclaimed Ortega. "It is much brighter than your moon in Texas, no?"

"Absolutely."

Men stood up to let them pass through the cars. The Yaqui commander, Arias, approached Ortega. He carried his saddle scabbard under his left arm, with the walnut stock of his Winchester protruding from it.

"Mi general," he said.

"Speak."

59

Arias began to pull the Winchester from its sheath. Arango instantly went into a combat crouch, his hand on his gun butt.

"*Mi treinta-treinta* is bewitched," Arias said with a troubled expression. Slocum thought the man was joking about his thirty-thirty, but it was clear that he was not. Arango recognized this immediately; his hand came away from his rifle stock reluctantly. Slocum knew it was because he had been denied a chance to kill.

"Oh?" said Ortega. His face was serious. It was obvious to Slocum that the Mexican was superstitious.

"*Si*. I missed everyone I shot at. This discontents and embarrasses me. My men laugh at me." He chewed his lower lip in annoyance. Arias's Winchester had silver ornaments set into its walnut stock. It had been seized from a wealthy rancher months ago, and Arias called it Lupita.

"A spirit sits astraddle of Lupita," he said seriously. "Right here. And every time I fire Lupita she jumps on the bullet and steers it to one side so that it will not hit anybody." His face had a worried expression. "And so I am ashamed."

"Stupid idiot," Arango said curtly. "Take one of the new Mausers." Arias flushed red.

Slocum moved back slightly. He did not want to be caught in any cross fire. But Arias turned aside and slowly slid the Winchester back into its scabbard. His hands were trembling. A shame, Slocum thought. Arias might have killed Arango, but even that brave Yaqui had backed away from a fight.

"*Capitán*," Slocum said.

Arias turned sullenly to face him.

"There are gunsmiths in Torreón," Slocum said. "The patron saint of gunsmiths will listen to your prayers, without doubt, especially if you will give a gift to the

60

Virgin before you go to the gunsmith. And if you would light a candle to the patron saint in the cathedral at Torreón—"

He paused. Arias's face lit up with joy. "*Sí!*" he said jubilantly, "*sí, sí!* Not one candle, *five* candles! Big ones!' He looked affectionately at Slocum.

Arango had turned and was staring out the open door without expression into the *chaparral* that flowed by endlessly. Even the rigid set of the man's back showed his dislike of Arias's warm approval of Slocum.

They continued on through the long line of train cars. When they stepped into the pullman, Ortega reached out and removed Arango's *sombrero*. Slocum had already removed his, and he stood for a second, enjoying Arango's annoyance as he held out a hand for his *sombrero*. Ortega thrust it roughly at him, shaking his head in faint disgust at Arango's lack of manners.

Slocum awaited her entry with interest. When she stepped through the heavy red velvet drapes that separated the bedroom area from the elaborately Victorian drawing room, he stared at her with appreciation. She wore a long sleek black gown. She was a beautiful woman. No wonder Ortega was so pleased with his possession. Ortega took a deep breath to savor her perfume, and as he did so he looked proudly at Slocum.

Slocum bowed. "Who is dead in heaven that the angels wear black?" he asked.

"*Qué lindo!*" said Ortega, dazzled with the compliment. Arango, as Slocum was careful to note, reacted with a thin, satisfied smile.

"Luis," Ortega said, "why don't you ever say anything as good as that?"

"I shall," Arango said. "But not now."

Ortega sighed. "Never mind," he said. "Let us have the brandy," he told her. She nodded, looking intently at Slocum before she turned toward a cabinet attached to the wall beside one of the windows. Arango smiled again, almost happily.

"My house is yours," Ortega said, indicating the chairs. He sat in one, stretching out his feet straight in front. His big roweled spurs rolled over the valuable Turkish rug, gouging out a few threads. Arango was equally careless. Slocum sat on the couch, carefully crossing his legs. He knew that most women regarded their physical environment—especially the furniture and rugs—as extensions of their bodies, and to treat furniture carelessly meant that you had a correspondingly low opinion of them.

She looked at him with a tight, controlled, yet approving, little smile. Slocum smiled back. She turned to withdraw, and Slocum saw that Arango was carefully filing away their exchange of smiles. She returned at once, carrying a tray with four glasses and an expensive cutglass decanter filled with a pale brown liquor.

"Hennessey," Ortega said nonchalantly, "very special old pale."

He behaved as if he had been drinking it all his life. She set the tray on an end table whose top was formed of an expensive ivory and rare wood inlay. She poured the brandy. Arango drank his immediately and held out his glass for more, before Ortega had even began to sip his.

"Luis!" Ortega said, disgusted. He shook his head.

"More!"

"Give him more," Ortega said, resigned. She poured another one. It went the same way and at the same speed as the previous drink. The train slowed. Ortega stood up and looked out the window. It was the first station south of Juárez with a telegraph operator. Ortega jerked his thumb. "Luis!" he said. Arango stood up, drained the last vestiges of brandy from his glass, and disappeared as the train ground to a halt. Three minutes later the train jerked and then began to move again. Ortega stood up again, pulled aside the curtain, and looked out. Satisfied, he grinned and let the curtain fall into place again. Arango stepped inside and nodded at Ortega.

"'*Sta bien*," he said. He sat down with his hat on. Ortega reached over, removed Arango's wide brimmed, gold-braided *sombrero* once more, and tossed it on a chair. He turned to Slocum.

"The telegraph is up from here to Torreón," he said. "At every station with a telegraph operator I am dropping off four men. One man in each group can read. Whenever a message comes from Torreón asking if they have seen a suspicious train, the operator will be careful to telegraph no, nothing suspicious. General Cisneros is in command of the train and all is well. The operators will be told if we find out later that they have sent any other message, the four men will come back and kill his family. It works. You will see. It works. We will be in Torreón about noon tomorrow. No more brandy for you, Luis. You will have to take care of all the telegraph operators all the rest of the night."

Once more Slocum felt admiration for Ortega's intelligence. Arango sat sullenly for a few minutes, staring at the brandy decanter. Then he abruptly stood up, grabbed his *sombrero*, and stalked out, his spurs clanking. He slammed the door behind him.

"Let him go," Ortega said placidly. "He will do his job. Ghislaine, *mi palomita*, will you please play solitaire with your ivory cards?"

She shrugged with a little tight smile of contempt around the corners of her mouth. "If it amuses you," she said. She pulled open a drawer in the inlaid table, removed the ivory discs, and began to place them in order on the table.

63

"Come closer for a better look," Ortega said, patting Slocum's knee. Slocum moved closer. His knee now touched hers, and she immediately responded with a faint, unmistakable return pressure. To this invitation Slocum did not respond. He wanted to live through the fore-seeable future. She pressed even more firmly, thinking that Slocum had not understood her gesture. She gazed at him for a second, a tight mocking smile tightening the corners of her pale rose lips. She was a little flushed with the brandy she had drunk. Slocum felt the heat of her body radiating through her dress onto his pants leg. She was in heat, just like a female dog, and just as unheeding and reckless. Ortega noticed nothing. He was fully absorbed in picking up an occasional disc not in play, rubbing it between his finger and thumb, marvel-ing at the decoration, and muttering, "Round cards, *round* cards!"

She was not behaving logically. Not only was Ortega in a position to give her food, comfort, and protection, but he—if well-handled by her, and she certainly looked like an expert—he might give her money and some of the jewelry he was planning to strip from the wives of the wealthy *gachupines* in Torreón. That was one point. The second point was that Ortega, if he found out that she was making him a cuckold, would kill her as casually as he would crush a cockroach under his boot heel. So why was she making this play for Slocum? Was she so bored with Ortega—and so careless of her life and her financial situation—that she would risk both, like a passionate gambler who didn't care if he was faced with a crooked roulette wheel, as long as it would spin in its unpredictable fashion?

Slocum liked the feel of her thigh pressing against his. He liked the faint aroma of her perfume—was it roses?—and the idea of watching her slowly pull her black dress up above her knees, up the length of her thighs until the dress went past her black silk-stocking tops, and traveled up her white thighs, up, up—the thought itself brought on an instant erection.

The train began to slow down. Ortega put down the beautifully carved queen of spades he was holding, and standing up, moved the curtain aside to see what the trouble was. There was no one else in the car. She kept her glance fastened on Ortega's back lest he should turn around suddenly. She calmly placed her palm on Slocum's hard penis. She stroked it gently and skillfully with the tips of her fingers, smiling as she looked at Ortega's back all the time. Ortega cursed and opened the window. He leaned out, demanding loudly to know what was happening up ahead. Someone yelled back that they had stopped at a water tower. Arias's voice floated up from the ground outside.

"*Mi general*," he called out, excited, "there is a shrine here to Guadalupita!"

"I'm coming," Ortega said. He pulled his shoulder back inside. When he turned, Ghislaine was demurely studying her cards.

"*Señor*," Ortega said, "would you care to leave an offering? It's the Virgin of Guadalupe. She will keep you from danger."

It was a fine opportunity to get away from Ghislaine without hurting her feelings. "I am not a Catholic," Slocum said.

"I shall see that she does not object," Ortega said with a wide grin. He led the way out. Slocum turned at the door for a last glance at Ghislaine. She was leaning back in a corner of the sofa, slowly swinging one black-stockinged leg back and forth. When she saw that he had turned around to look at her, she ran a palm over her breasts, smiling. Maybe she was worth running a risk for, Slocum mused, but, to lose a *railroad concession* over a woman? No, it did not make any kind of sense whatsoever. He resolutely went down the steps to do business with the Virgin of Guadalupe, a much more sensible relationship.

15

Guadalupita had been crudely carved out of oak. She was three feet tall and had been exposed to the sun and occasional rain for over 70 years. She stood serenely on her pedestal, which in turn had been nailed on top of a four-inch square of timber, sunk firmly into the hard-packed clay soil. A large tin cup was nailed to the base of the carving at her feet. Below that someone had tied a chipped glass vase to the upright post. By the time Slocum had arrived, several men had crammed road-side flowers into it, in lieu of cash.

Arias was kneeling in front of the statue, his *sombrero* on the ground beside him. He next crossed himself, stood up, and dropped two *pesos* into the cup. Many others were kneeling and praying in a circle around the Virgin.

"Our Virgin is very powerful," Ortega said proudly. "I prayed to her before we went into Juárez. She appreciates our gifts. She likes the money as well as the flowers. Perhaps more, who can say?"

Slocum dropped two *pesos* inside the cup.

Slocum was not sure whether Ortega believed this, or whether he said it in order to maintain the loyalty of his undoubtedly superstitious men. All of them, after notic-ing that their general was praying, had jumped off the train. They were kneeling and muttering prayers. Ortega now stood up, briskly slapped his dusty knees with his *sombrero*, and called out, *"Vamonos, chicos, adelante a Torreón!"*

The men began to climb aboard, chatting happily. The tin cup was overflowing with coins. One Yaqui, who had lost all his money gambling and who had not been able to find any flowers because all near the Virgin had been picked and jammed into the glass vase, had simply deposited a *tortilla* at the base of the post.

"Won't the money be stolen?" Slocum asked as they walked back to the pullman.

"My friend," Ortega said, "we have given the money to the Virgin. It is now hers to dispose of any way she wants. If she wants to give it to some poor *peon* who needs it to sustain life or buy fireworks for a *fiesta*, I do not object. And if the priest takes it for the church, she will also be happy. But not so happy. *'Sta bien.* She will take care of us in Torreón. You will see." He turned and began to climb aboard.

Slocum hoped so. Maybe if the southern armies in his Civil War had done the same at every roadside shrine —if there had been any such shrines—would Second Manassas have turned out differently? He was smiling at the thought as he put his foot on the bottom step of the pullman. He climbed one step and sensed someone was blocking his path. He looked up. Arango.

The train began to move. Arango did not stir.

"*Con su permiso,*" Slocum said politely, concealing the hot sensation of anger that instantly filled him.

Arango pointed alongside the track. "Look, *gringo,*" he said triumphantly. Slocum turned his head and looked where Arango was pointing. Two silver discs lay on the gravel.

"Your *pesos,*" Arango said, grinning. His right thumb was hooked into his gun belt and his right palm was flat against his thigh. All he had to do was pivot his hand at the wrist and it would fall easily onto his gun butt. Whereas Slocum's hands were grasping the vertical railings on each side of the steps. "Your *pesos,*" Arango repeated. "They offended the Virgin."

"She threw them out?"

"*Sí*," Arango said pleasantly.

"You saw her do it, no doubt."

"With my own eyes. I swear it." He lifted his left hand high, as if he were taking an oath. His right hand did not move a fraction of an inch away from his Colt.

Slocum felt rage rising within him, like lava oozing upward. His head was at the level of Arango's stomach. He could ram his head deep into the man's solar plexus and thus temporarily paralyze him so that he would not be able to pull the Colt. But it might not work. Slocum had once seen a man with two bullets in his brain draw and fire four shots before he went down, dead, taking one of his murderers with him to hell. The risk was too much, especially with a fine shot like Arango. Once more he persuaded himself that he had come to Mexico to protect an investment and not to accept challenges to his sense of honor.

"*Que pasa?*" demanded Ortega. The general had come back to see what was keeping them on the steps while the train was picking up speed.

"We're talking, *mi general*," Arango said.

"On the steps?" Ortega's voice was skeptical.

"On the steps," Slocum said calmly.

Ortega looked from one man's face to the other's. He felt the tension and settled the affair quickly.

"Luis, I don't like that stupid idiot you put on the throttle. You drive it."

"But——"

"Luis. *Drive* it."

"*Sí, mi general.*" Arango reluctantly turned and made his way forward. Ortega stared hard at Slocum's face. Suddenly he demanded, "What happened?"

"A small difference of opinion. Nothing serious."

"With Arango, my friend, there is no such thing as a small difference. All differences are serious with that man."

The train was moving faster now. The moon had begun its climb to the night sky's zenith, and the distant mountains looked like a jumbled pile of gently rounded silver ingots. There had been a brief early local shower in that part of Chihuahua where they were now traveling, and as the train chugged on into the night, the fragrance of the wet sagebrush blew across the tracks.

"Why keep him?" Slocum suddenly demanded.

Ortega looked at him with a surprised expression. "Because he's very good with railroads," he said simply. "Also, he hates Díaz. And he is very good with the Yaquis. It is hard to command Indians. They are very cruel and *they* are scared of him. Let us all get some sleep. Tomorrow we will be in battle."

Slocum nodded. He said good night and picked his way toward the rear to the express car where he had spread his blankets. He kicked off his boots, tipped his *sombrero* over his face, but he still found it hard to go to sleep, even though he was very tired. He was still simmering with hatred for Arango. He could only fall asleep by promising himself that when it was all over he would settle the score with *Capitán* Luis. The thought eased his mind and he dropped off to sleep to the rhythmic *clackety-clack-clack* of the wheels. He dozed on and off. Once he woke up and saw that the sun had risen. He fell asleep, but woke again when the rhythm of the wheels had changed to a very slow *clack-clack-clack*. They were moving at ten miles an hour around a hairpin curve in a very narrow defile. Just as he was idly thinking that it was the perfect place for an ambush, he heard two violent explosions, one in front of the locomotive and one behind the last car.

Someone else had thought it was the perfect place for an ambush.

16

The federals had buried two dynamite charges in the roadbed; one blew the tracks in front and the second took care of the rear, so that the train could not reverse. This accomplished, the train hissed to a stop as Arango frantically braked the locomotive. The federals then quickly fired 50 rounds from their French mountain artillery into the troop-carrying cars at point-blank range.

As soon as Slocum heard the first explosions, he threw off his blanket, pulled on his boots, buckled on his gun belt, grabbed his Winchester, and pushed open the sliding door all the way. He jumped down. A shadowy figure rose up out of the dark drainage ditch and swung a rifle at his head. Slocum saw it coming down at him, but too late. Only his *sombrero* saved him from a fractured skull. He groaned and pitched forward, unconscious before he struck the ground.

A bucket of water struck him in the face. He opened his eyes. He was lying on his back in a garden. The sun was low, so he knew it was late afternoon—as long as it was not the next day. His head ached badly. Ten feet away there sat a federal officer in his blue uniform in an armchair. The armchair rested on the flagstones of a veranda in the shade. Slocum was in the sun. He was very thirsty. He ran a tongue around his cracked lips and looked at the officer. Like Cisneros, he had the closely cropped pompadour of the officer class, but this man was much fatter, and he had a bushy mustache.

Slocum tried to move. His wrists were tied together in the small of his back and they gouged painfully into his spine whenever he moved. His boots, gun belt, and *sombrero* were gone. The spoils of war, he thought ruefully. One day mine, next day theirs. He turned his head and licked at the grass, trying to moisten his mouth.

"Thirsty, you *gringo* son of a bitch?"

The officer was talking. Slocum did not look at him. The officer's voice sounded smug and self-satisfied, as if he were mightily pleased with himself. One thing at a time, Slocum thought. If he were to ask for water, he might not get it. Better to take it whenever he could. The few drops he managed to lick up from the drenched grass made his parched mouth feel slightly better.

"Your name is Mitchell, no?"

"No."

"I think it is, *señor*."

"No. It is Andrew Hancock."

"You are a liar, *señor*."

"I am sorry you think so."

The officer snapped his fingers. An orderly ran up with a box of cigars and opened it. The officer selected one. The soldier closed the box, struck a match and waited anxiously until the officer grunted approval. Then he withdrew. The officer inhaled luxuriously.

"Do you smoke?"

"Occasionally, *señor*."

The officer leaned forward and blew smoke at Slocum. Then he leaned back. "Let us introduce ourselves," he said. "My name is Colonel Ramon O'Conor Escalante. You are in the house of *Don* Aurelio Gutierrez. He is a good friend of mine. He has agreed to be your host. Yes, this is your house. Now, have I lied to you?"

"Probably not," said Slocum calmly, wondering where the hell all this was leading to.

"Good. What is your name?"

"Andrew Hancock."

71

The colonel sighed. "I told you the truth," he said reproachfully, "and you lied to me. What were you doing on the train?"

"I was in El Paso, offering money to buy Mexican cattle," Slocum said easily, with all the direct stare he could summon up in a supine position. "I wanted to stock ranches in Wyoming. A man spoke to me and said he could supply a few thousand Mexican cattle. He took me to Juárez. There I was taken to a train. There was a man on the train called, I think, Ortega. He said if I would come with him, and wait a week, or ten days, he would sell me all the cattle I wanted, at a very low price. It looked somewhat illegal, and I thought he scarcely looked the part of a rancher—still, in this business, one buys cattle where one can."

"Who is the man you spoke to in El Paso?"

"He called himself Arango—Luis Arango."

"You seem to have a military bearing, *señor*. Are you a mercenary?"

"No. I am a cattle buyer. But I was an officer in the American Civil War for four years."

"Ah?" Escalante said, intrigued. "What rank?"

"In a lieutenant, out a major."

"What branch?"

"Cavalry."

"So. Would you like to know what happened to your train and your friends?"

"It was not my train. They were not my friends."

"I know, *señor*. You were, as you say, a cattle buyer, who *happened* to be on the train. But it was not a passenger train. One could only be on it by invitation?"

"That's right."

"Or by inclination."

Slocum shrugged. "One buys cattle where one can," he said. "Especially when they are cheap and there's a good market for them."

72

"How could you buy cattle?"

"With money."

"What money?"

Slocum was resigned to the loss of the money in his money belt. The gold would back up his story and would save his life. He would never see it again, however. Nevertheless, it would be wise to sacrifice it.

"Here," he said, jerking his chin downwards. "In my money belt." As soon as he said it he realized that the money belt was gone. He felt sick.

Escalante snapped an order. The orderly stepped down from the veranda, bent down, and ripped Slocum's shirt open.

"I told you you were a liar, *señor*."

"Colonel. Search your men. Find someone with plenty of American 20-dollar gold pieces. Ask him to explain them."

"How much in gold?"

Slocum told him. The colonel looked at him thoughtfully. He gave orders. The orderly withdrew.

"Do you know what happened to your train, *señor*?"

"No."

"*I* destroyed it!" He stood with a proud, contemplative smile. "Yes. I may very well write it up for the *Revue Militaire*. It was a classic ambush." He sighed with pleasure at the memory. He proceeded to tell Slocum about it.

"President Díaz knew you were coming. His agents in Brownsville and El Paso kept him posted. So he decided not to oppose Ortega in the north. If he won a battle against Ortega, then the *bandido* and his men would simply run to the United States once more. And try again. So he ordered me to let Ortega do whatever he wanted. We pulled out almost all our troops in Chihuahua. Ortega took the depot in Juárez. The bank surprised us. But it was good; it made Ortega over-confident. And sure enough, Ortega worked himself very deeply into Mexico.

"Troops have blocked all the roads and railroads to the north. We let Ortega come down this far because we knew he wanted Torreón. We waited for you just north of the town. You do not have an army anymore. We have patrols out looking for the very few who did escape; we'll get them all." The colonel drew a forefinger across his throat.

More than anything else, Slocum would like a long, long drink of cold water. He thought his only chance to live would be that somehow his United States double eagles would turn up hidden in some soldier's gear. He felt regret that the venture had ended disastrously, but that was the key problem with high-profit situations: They were always accompanied by high risk.

He took a chance. "Water, please," he said.

"Why not?" said Escalante genially. He turned and spoke softly toward a room into which Slocum could not see because of the violent sunlight in his eyes. Slocum heard bare feet padding on the stones. Half a minute later the padding came again. It was a barefoot Indian maid carrying a tray with a glass pitcher full of water, a plate heaped high with slices of limes, and a glass. The colonel squeezed half a lime into the glass and then poured it full.

"Cold well water," he said. He proceeded to drink it slowly. "Mmmm," he murmured. "Delicious! You don't look very well. How do you feel?"

" 'The week begins badly for a man who is hung on Monday,' " Slocum said, quoting the proverb.

The colonel slapped his thigh and chuckled. "Very good," he said approvingly. The orderly appeared, and, slipping behind the colonel's chair, bent down and whispered briefly. The colonel nodded regretfully.

"I am sorry to say that you are a liar, *señor*," he said.

"I will have to torture you for more information than you are willing to give me. My men, in an excess of praiseworthy enthusiasm, forgot to take prisoners. But before we begin, would you care for a drink of water?"

Slocum regretted his next action. He had thought that the colonel was serious this time, and so he nodded. The colonel stood up, moved closer, and threw the glass and its contents into Slocum's face. The face of Escalante convulsed with sudden rage, but it was an open rage. Slocum felt the same wild and furious hatred, but he kept his face impassive; an expression of anger on his part would have pleased the colonel, and Slocum did not want to do anything to win the colonel's approval. The little Indian orderly stood behind the colonel, with his Mauser slung across his back. Escalante turned quickly, seized the rifle, drove a cartridge into the chamber, and fired it between Slocum's legs.

"*Desgraciado cabrón!*" he shouted out of control. His face had swollen in fury, like a turkey's comb. His eyes bulged and his face was sweating, even in the cool air of the veranda. "*You* bought those rifles in El Paso! *You* bought the horses! Lying bastard!"

Slocum's head was splitting. The loud explosion in the *patio* had made it ache even more, and the impact of the heavy bullet into the soil between his upper thighs had created a sharp, sudden shock which he felt in his testicles. He saw the frightened faces of the Indian maids appear at the French windows opening onto the veranda. Escalante turned and tossed the Mauser to the orderly. Then he spun around and walked quickly away.

Jesus, that was *close*, Slocum thought. His heart gradually resumed its normal pace. He closed his eyes. He had eaten nothing since supper the day before; but he felt the thirst much more than the hunger. He heard the colonel's boots click quickly across the flagstones of the veranda, then the slam of a door. The little orderly

75

bent down and whispered. *"Señor,"* he said with admiration, *"tiene huevos."*

So he had balls, Slocum thought. That last shot had come close to eliminating them. And he might not have them for long. He nodded and said, *"Agua?"* The orderly shook his head regretfully and resumed his guard position on the veranda.

Slocum looked around carefully. It would be important for him to know the layout of the place like the palm of his hand. He was inside the *patio* of a great rambling mansion. There were two fountains, both of them too far away to do him any good. The walls surrounding the *patio* were very high, at least 30 feet, he judged, with three-foot-wide tops, and massive amounts of broken glass set viciously on edge. Two iron gates formed the entrance. He could see two soldiers lounging in the street just outside the gates. They would be the sentries on duty. Flowers bloomed everywhere: in pots set along the edge of the veranda, all along the base of the wall, all along the edges of the walks through the *patio*. Great masses of purple bougainvillea climbed the pillars which supported the house wherever it extended above the veranda.

The flowers were at their lushest near the fountains, because the wind would blow the spray over the flowers. The idea of being tortured in the midst of such fragrances brought a wry smile to Slocum's face. He hoped he would be able to stand it.

Escalante came back with another soldier. "Up, up!" he commanded. Slocum struggled to his knees but was unable to stand. Then the soldiers pulled him erect and supported him.

"Imbeciles!" said the colonel. "Come here!" They let Slocum slip to the ground. They stood in front of their officer with puzzled expressions on their brown peasant faces. He pointed to their Mausers, still slung around

76

their chests. They sheepishly removed them and handed them to the colonel, who brought up the rear, and they hoisted Slocum to his feeble feet and began walking inside the house.

But Slocum knew that even if he had succeeded in seizing one of the Mausers—and the thought had occurred to him—he still would have been too weak and too slow to have been able to rip it off anyone's chest. The soldiers whispered "*Adelantito*," just a little way ahead, in order to encourage him. They crossed a floor made of Durango tile, on which was a carpet in red and blue. He could see huge French windows opening onto a balcony which ran the length of the enormous room. Above the top rail of the balcony he could see the branches of old, massive ahuehuete trees, which so much resembled the familiar cottonwoods of Slocum's familiar Southwest. There were canaries in elaborate wire cages and little boxes scattered on the tables, holding Mexican cigarettes. Heavy Victorian couches in mahogany were placed at regular intervals along the edges of the room. A fireplace big enough for a grown man to stand in was set into the far corner of the room, with neatly sawn logs piled up at the foot of the wall, ready for chilly evenings. Near the fireplace was a vast, canopied bed, festooned around the edges with Belgian lace. The entire bed was covered with great folds of mosquito netting, and, sitting cross-legged in dead center, buffing her nails, was Ghislaine Marchand.

17

"*Mademoiselle.*"

"*Monsieur le Colonel.*" She did not stop buffing her nails. She looked at Slocum without expression.

"Do you know this man?"

She stared at Slocum. After a moment she said calmly, "Yes."

"Who is he?"

"He is an American."

"What was he doing on your train?"

Slocum felt fear chilling his belly.

"He was a good friend of General Ortega's," she said with a faint smile. "He bought horses and rifles for the general. He gave advice."

That did it, Slocum knew. His last chance and she had coldly eliminated it. This was the end.

"What kind of advice?"

"Oh, how to take the depot, how to take Torreón, things like that."

"Strategic and tactical matters?"

"I'm not sure what you mean."

Whether she knew what the words meant or not, Slocum knew, she was very efficiently digging his grave. Perhaps he should have responded to her open invitation on the train the night before. Had he done so, he was sure that his present situation would now be much more favorable. He shrugged. It was too late now. He had learned a little more about women, but it wasn't going to be of any practical use this time. He took a good look at her. She did look very tasty, he decided. It was going to be his last look at a woman, and at least she was beautiful, seen through the pale mist of the mosquito netting, as she sat in a filmy white gown with her long hair piled up in a concentric swirl atop her head.

On the other side of the bed was a blue enamel pan on a cane tripod, and in the pan were two champagne bottles resting on a bed of cracked ice. The ice had half-melted, and the bottom half of the pan held water. She saw his eyes yearning for it. Slocum knew that a word from her to the colonel and she would ask for the water to be given to him—and there was a good chance he would relent that much. She slowly shook her head. Time to say good-bye to her.

"*Puta,*" he said, his voice hoarse because of his parched throat.

"You earn your way through the world, *amigo mío,*" she said calmly, "and so do I."

There was a tap on the door.

"*Pase!*" said the colonel.

The door opened. "Ah, *Don* Aurelio," Escalante said. "You have come to see your guest? He would say that your hospitality has been magnificent. As for me, I would swear to that."

"*Tiro la casa por la ventana,*" Slocum heard a pleasant voice announce. "I throw the house out the window." Slocum had never heard the old-fashioned Spanish phrase expressing hospitality. *Don* Aurelio Gutierrez was a plump, balding man with a shaggy mustache.

"It is a great pleasure."

"I am happy to give it to you, my dear colonel. The barracks in Torreón are vile, vile! The officers' quarters are not even passable. And anything you can do to eliminate the vermin from the North who come down to loot the *haciendas* is, I assure you, deeply appreciated."

The colonel made some polite, deprecatory sounds.

"No, no, I insist. Mexico is becoming a country we can be proud of. And the credit is due to *Don* Porfi."

Slocum had never heard this affectionate manner of referring to Díaz. He listened with interest; they seemed to have temporarily forgotten his presence.

"A most astute statesman. He stayed in this very room two years ago. Not realizing, of course, that a charming lady from France would be sleeping in his very bed." He bowed. She smiled. "He encourages investment, builds railroads—and how else could I send my beef and my

79

mineral ores to market? And my sugar from Cuautla? He has been very helpful in securing Yaquis to work in my *henequén* plantations in Yucatán."

"I would have liked to supply some more this morning," Escalante said. "But my gunners were too enthusiastic."

"I very well understand you could not take any chances with that lot."

"Precisely."

"I heard there was an American mercenary with Ortega. Is this true or is it a rumor?"

"It is true, *Don* Aurelio. He is lying in the corner there."

Gutierrez turned and stared with curiosity at Slocum. "I am about to persuade him to talk," Escalante said. "Would it amuse you to watch?"

"No, in heaven's name, Colonel, no."

A sensitive fellow, Slocum thought. Gutierrez opened his waistcoat, slid his hands inside his back pockets and, pretending to stare at Slocum, was, in reality, looking Ghislaine over very carefully. "These things are necessary, Colonel, but, alas, to be deplored. A sensible man can always find a better occupation than fighting. I have always busied myself with regular industry. The North Americans understand that. They always have good ideas. Without money in his pocket, what is a man good for? He might as well take himself over to the cemetery and have done with it."

"Umm," said the colonel. It was clear to Slocum that the colonel took a dim view of *Don* Aurelio's philosophy, but then, he was a guest in his very comfortable house.

"However," *Don* Aurelio went on, "soldiers are necessary to protect what we build for. I do not decry the military, you understand—we are both the pillars that support the state—and I fully approve of what *Don* Porfi is doing for the army, and of his policy to root out

80

these animals from the North. But, Colonel, you look somewhat tired."

"I am, *Don* Aurelio. I have had a long day. I must get to work."

Gutierrez was silent.

"Er—" he said, with a troubled voice, "will there be any—ah—noise?"

"No. You have a storeroom somewhere?"

"Yes. Below."

"Thick walls, of coures?"

"Yes."

"You will not be disturbed, I assure you. And, afterwards, I will retire."

"Of course! And enjoy the spoils of war. What a magnificent woman!" He bowed toward Ghislaine, who inclined her head half an inch. "I envy you, Colonel. It is lucky my wife is away visiting friends in Paris, or she would accuse me of staring too hard at *Mademoiselle* Marchand."

"It is time to get to work, *Don* Aurelio."

"Will there be any—er—mess?"

"If there is, my men will leave the room immaculate. They are trained for it."

"Good. Would you and the lady care to have breakfast with me?"

"Delighted, my dear *Don* Aurelio."

What a civilized conversation, Slocum thought. He hoped he would not make a mess.

A few minutes later he was in a dark room in the cellar. There were no windows, only a single massive oak door with a six-inch-square opening in the top half, with a bar in the center. It was big enough to pass food through. It looked as if it had been designed for a storeroom, but had been converted into a prison cell. There was nothing in the room whatsoever, except an iron bar projecting from the wall at right angles, obviously some device on which to hang a lantern—and a small chamber pot.

The colonel removed a big key from his jacket pocket, unlocked the door, and stood aside while his two men dragged Slocum inside. They propped him against the wall under the iron bar. One of the men now produced a rawhide *reata*, shaking out the loop, and placed it over Slocum's head. The cold, rough leather clung tightly to his neck as the shorter soldier tightened the loop.

Here it comes, Slocum thought. Here's where I die. In a basement in Mexico. No one will ever know what happened to me. The next day my body will be thrown into a *barranca*, and by sundown the *zapilotes* will have stripped all the flesh. He had taken a chance and lost. There would be no begging for his life on his part. He would have liked very much to drink a cold glass of milk.

"Pull," Escalante said.

Slocum went up in the air. After seven seconds Escalante motioned for him to be lowered.

"Has your memory improved?"

"Go to hell," is what Slocum wanted to say but, only a thin reedy squawk emerged from his contracted throat muscles. Slocum knew that if he did tell the truth his death would follow immediately. Díaz was not well known for mercy to anyone who willfully aided a rebel. Slocum's only hope was to keep the pretense that he was only an innocent cattle buyer, and that Escalante would think that maybe the Frenchwoman was somehow making a mistake in identification. It was all that Slocum had to cling to.

"Once more," Escalante said. "Slowly."

Slocum tried to stiffen his neck muscles in order to take some of the strain off his windpipe. The rawhide closed around his neck like a coil of red-hot barbed wire. His consciousness started to cloud as the blood supply to his brain was shut off. The thought came to Slocum that he was glad it was not Arango, who was doing the hoisting up and down; somehow he did not think that Escalante would have taken the same pleasure in the act that Arango would have. It was a minor comfort.

"*Abajo.*"

Down he slid again. His body slumped against the wall, and his head tilted to one side because of the pressure of the rope.

"Where is Arango? Where is Ortega? Where did you arrange to meet?"

So! They got away!

"*Arriba!*"

Up he went again. He did not think he could hold on any more. There was no point. He knew he might hold on a bit more, but to what purpose? If he would make up a story about the rendezvous point where he would meet Ortega and Arango, what would an innocent rancher be doing with such information? It would be immediate proof of his complicity in the rebellion, and he would gain nothing by it. So, Slocum thought, if he were to die, better to become unconscious first and avoid the last horrible aborted clutchings at his throat—the same kind of thing he had seen many times when he had hung bushwhackers he had caught raping and murdering innocent farm women during the Civil War. For a second he formulated his epitaph: *I did what I wanted*; *no regrets*. Then blackness.

18

Someone was slapping his face. He opened his eyes. A lantern was still burning in the hook attached to the wall. A face was bending over him. He braced himself for a blow. But something was out of the ordinary here, and it took a couple of seconds to realize what it was: He smelled perfume. Then he knew: It was Ghislaine Marchand.

"Can you hear me?" she whispered. He nodded.

She held up the key. "The colonel is drunk," she said triumphantly. "The guards are drunk. They're all celebrating their great victory. He's snoring. He drank both bottles. He thinks he's very intelligent. He told me exactly how he won the battle. Do you want to know how?"

"I want water."

She went away and came back with a pitcher full of the cool well water Slocum remembered from the afternoon before. Slocum had enough control to take it in small sips until he had enough.

"You'll be able to escape by climbing down over the balcony railing and along the branch of that big tree. Would you like that?"

"Yes." Slocum wondered what the hell kind of a game she was playing, with that idiotic question.

"But there's one condition."

Here it comes, Slocum thought. "Yes," he said calmly.

"I find you a very attractive man." Here she keeps on talking, he thought angrily, and all he wanted was to get away before any of the guards woke up! But he knew he would have to handle the crazy bitch carefully. It was his only chance to live.

"And?" Slocum asked. His voice came out as a thin croak, his throat was very painful, and each swallow had made him wince. For the first time he noticed a large woven basket behind her. She pulled out a napkin which had been wrapped around something. She unwrapped it; it covered a large roast chicken. The smell of it made his mouth water.

"You understand my condition?"

"Of course," he croaked. Swallowing was painful. But he ate, savoring each mouthful of the firm, garlic-scented meat. In a few minutes he felt strength flowing back into his body, as if it were a reservoir filling. She sat cross-legged on the floor, her elbows perched on her knees, watching him eat, with her thin, contemplative smile.

Oh, he thought, eating, this is a *gran puta*, all right. She had hitched up her skirt, and she calmly stared at him as his gaze involuntarily dropped down to her bare thighs and her crotch. She made no attempt to cover herself.

To his surprise he felt his penis stir. He had thought nothing could happen after his hanging experience and his fatigue. When he had eaten, she produced a fine linen napkin. Slocum was amused to observe that *Don* Aurelio lived well, even if the man would be indignant if he knew what was happening to his fine table linen. Slocum wiped his greasy hands. She took it from him, poured some water on it from the pitcher, wiped his face, and gently rubbed his hands. Slocum winced when she slid the damp napkin over his wrists, which were still painfully swollen from the excessive tightness of the bonds. That done, she replaced the napkin and from the basket withdrew a half-full bottle of champagne.

"Only take a couple sips," she warned, "the stupid colonel drank too much and could not perform."

Slocum grinned. For her the world was divided into two kinds of men: those who had money and those who could perform. The idea was to find a man with both essentials. If this proved impossible, she would take the former and search hungrily for the latter—and this, obviously, at great personal risk to herself if she should be discovered. Slocum knew that she was very much like him—if her game was exposed, she would not cry for mercy. He respected that quality.

"What are you smiling at?" she demanded furiously. "I have no time to waste. Hurry up and take off your clothes!"

Slocum pointed out that he hadn't bathed for days. "No matter, no matter," she said hungrily, "the colonel wears perfume and I didn't care for Ortega in any way. Quick, now!"

She helped him pull off his shirt and unbuckle his belt. He stood up and unsteadily balanced himself against the wall with one hand. She helped him pull off his pants. While he stood there, she reached up and caressed his penis with her fingertips, with very gentle touches, like the beating of butterfly wings. After a minute nothing had happened, much to his embarrassment. She looked up and smiled as she cupped it in both palms. Slocum understood her smile: She had been through this before with many of her customers, and her smile had the look of a competent technician faced with what looked like, at first glance, to be a serious problem. But it was a serious problem only for an amateur. For an expert like her, it was as easy as rolling off a log. She bent forward and took him in her mouth, working with great skill.

It was no use. After three minutes, she gave up and sat back on her heels with a look of utter disgust, relinquishing her grip on him. Slocum thought that her expression indicated a strong wish to throw it to the *zapilotes*, and he was embarrassed more than ever. But still, the combination of fatigue, the effect of even a small amount of alcohol on an exhausted body, the pain from his swollen wrists, where the flesh was puffed up to an angry red, and the knowledge that there were people very close who would like to kill him—these created a conviction in Slocum that he was not seriously at fault. Still, he knew the futility of explaining this to most women, and particularly to a woman like Ghislaine Marchand. More than anything else, Slocum wanted to get out of there. He watched her as she angrily replaced everything in the basket. In spite of her annoyance, he felt he owed her gratitude for the great risk she had run. Still, he would have preferred just to say *muchas gracias* and then get the hell out of there fast. There were just too many factors inhibiting his usually strong, powerful reaction to a beautiful woman who had attracted him. But all of this was something he could not mention to that impetuous, headstrong and eccentric woman.

She rose to her feet and moved to the door. She looked at him, placed a forefinger to her pale-rose lips, and peered out through the small grating. Then she quietly unlocked the door. Slocum stood up painfully and waited. She opened the door and set the basket in the hallway outside. Slocum began moving toward her. She suddenly held up her hand in a warning gesture. He froze. She slid out and closed the door. Ah, Slocum thought, I am to wait till she disappears. The next thing he heard was the sound of the key turning in the lock. He made a frantic leap to the door and pushed, but it was too late. He was locked in once more.

Slocum understood. If he had successfully screwed her, she would have let him out, and made up some story so that the risk of her being caught would not exist. Slocum trusted her intelligence enough to know that she would have probably gotten away with whatever story she made up. But if he didn't make love to her, what compensation would she be getting? None. Therefore, he could die in that cell, after torture, for all she cared.

All this passed through his mind almost instantaneously. He was at the door in three long strides, disregarding the pain in his swollen ankles. His hand slid through the little grating. She had half-turned away, but Slocum's right hand, strengthened by years of hard rope work, caught her by the throat. She brought both hands up and

87

tried to pry his hand loose by digging her long nails into the back of his palm. But by this time he had squeezed his other arm through and both hands completely encircled her slender neck. He squeezed a little bit, as a hint, and then relaxed his grip slightly, allowing her to breathe. She brought up both her hands again and raked the backs of both his hands with her sharp fingernails. It was painful, especially since her nails laid open some of the swollen flesh around his wrists. He squeezed her throat for four seconds. He did it gently; he did not want to fracture her larynx.

"Key," he whispered softly.

She gurgled and pointed downwards with a forefinger. She had dropped the key into her basket. He relaxed his hands.

"I'll get it," she gasped. "You'll have to let me loose. I swear I'll unlock the door." Slocum saw absolutely no reason in the world why he should trust her. "I swear to God," she said, her voice full of sincerity.

He could feel her throat vibrate against his palms as she spoke. If he were to shift his grip to her clothes to permit her to bend down to get the key out of the basket, she would probably tear herself out of his grip quite easily. Keeping one hand around the front of her throat, he pulled the back of her head hard against the grating. She was not able to move her head a fraction of an inch. Then, with his other hand, he pulled out all her hairpins. They fell to the stone floor with a faint, dry rattle. When he had removed them all, he took the topmost coil of her hair from her head and wrapped it around his palm three times. It was like dallying a steer around his saddle horn. There was no way she could now break away from that grip, and she knew it.

"Get it," he said. She sensed the steel in his voice. She squatted down and got the key.

"Unlock."

He relaxed his grip enough for her to be able to turn around. She turned the key in the lock. When he heard the mechanism sliding back, he pushed the door. It moved. He let her hair slip from his palm. There was one good thing about all this, Slocum silently observed: She wasn't going to scream for help. Even for her, it would be too hard to explain what she was doing down there with a basket with a champagne bottle, a napkin smeared with chicken stains, and a key. He took her inside.

"Take off your skirt," he said coldly.

She knew better than to argue. She stepped out of it silently. He pulled it on; he couldn't fasten it around his larger waist, but he adjusted the sash over the opening. He took her *rebozo* and slung it around his shoulders. Then he turned to face her. Her face was white and set hard. She would not beg. In many ways, Slocum thought, she was very much like him. He sighed and extended his hands. She stepped back. He followed her until he had boxed her in a corner. She raised her arms, ready to scratch in silence till the end, but Slocum's intentions were not what she feared.

He suddenly grabbed her right elbow, spun her around, and choked her into unconsciousness. Then he picked her up, slung her over a shoulder, picked up the basket, and left, locking the door behind him. He padded quietly down the hall, moving as quietly as an Indian maid. If he would be seen carrying only the basket, and if he would wear the *rebozo* over his head and shoulders, he could be taken in the dim light, at a distance, as a maid on an errand.

He climbed the stairs to the patio floor. He padded along the veranda and across the tile floor to her bed. At some distance he could hear the colonel's stertorous, drunken snoring. Satisfied, Slocum placed the still unconscious woman beside the colonel. He set the key inside the colonel's blue tunic, which was carelessly tossed over a chair next to the bed. He put the basket down, opened a dresser drawer, and crumpled up three bedsheets and placed them inside the basket. He picked up three sofa cushions and opened the door, then turned for one last look at the beautiful *Mademoiselle* Marchand. She was still unconscious. In the morning, Slocum knew, the squeezing he had given her around her neck would show up as ugly reddish-blue smears; it was her insurance policy, and it would save her life. An astute woman like Marchand would be sharp-witted enough to utilize that.

He was sure it would get her off the hook. After all, in spite of her unhelpful attitude when she said he had been a confederate of Ortega's, she had—unwittingly, it was true—helped him to escape. One deed balanced the other, so he was, in a sense, starting from scratch with her. She moaned suddenly. It would not do for her to open her eyes now. She might remember how he was dressed and pass on the information. Or, in her dazed condition, she might start screaming. He decided to do one more favor for her. He made a fist and hit her on the side of her jaw. It would leave a nice mark and render her definitely unconscious until he had left the building; it would also make her story more convincing.

He adjusted the *rebozo* until his head and torso were covered. The night air was chilly, and this was the traditional manner of wearing it at such times. He picked up three pillows and hung the basket on his left elbow. He padded barefoot down the hall, crossed the *patio*, and was about to go through the gate when he suddenly remembered the hairpins. If they were found by someone else in the morning, she would find that little thing difficult to explain. Too difficult, perhaps.

He turned and went back again, across the *patio*, and down into the storeroom. He picked them up, tossed them in the basket, went back up the stairs, and across the *patio* once more. In the stillness, the fountains splashed and gurgled. As Slocum approached the gate once more, he deliberately made his bare feet slap loudly on the flagstones.

Two soldiers sat cross-legged in front of the gate, their Mausers balanced across their knees. As he approached, they turned. They reacted the way Slocum thought they would: the maid, on her way to early market and selling a few of Aurelio's pillows.

One guard stood, opened the gate, and said, "Give me a little kiss."

Slocum whispered, "*Momentito.*"

The other guard slapped the first man on his back in congratulation on his unexpected conquest. The first man, grinning, poked the barrel of his Mauser under the bottom of Ghislaine's skirt and began to lift it. There was enough light pouring down from the half-moon in the sky to reveal a hairy leg if the dress would travel more than a few inches.

Slocum let one hand go from its grip on the pillows and slapped the man's face. Not too hard, just the right amount of energy a strong peasant girl might expend in that situation.

It was still a ringing slap and stung the man, who let out a surprised "*Puta!*" while the other soldier laughed. Had the soldier been alone, he would have hit back, but the presence of the other man forced him to accept the blow. He lowered his rifle barrel, recovered, and said cheerfully, as Slocum padded past him clutching the sofa pillows to his face and chest, "Ay, what strong legs! I want them locked around my back, little rabbit!"

Slocum moved into the darkness. When he was safely around the corner, he dropped everything, hoisted his skirt, and ran as hard as he could for five minutes. But he had aroused too many of the starved mongrels, which, having roamed the streets at night, now closed in on him.

They began barking frantically at his passage and approach. Slocum slowed to a walk. The dogs still followed, snarling. This would not do. He stopped and pried up one of the cobblestones and cracked the leader of the group in his ribs. The dog, in mid-snarl, immediately changed his noise to a pained yelp. The dogs stopped and let Slocum continue.

With that pressure removed, Slocum slowed down to think. He was barefoot, in women's clothes—which he could get away with at night, but never during daylight —500 miles deep inside a strange country, without a *peso*, with a lot of angry soldiers who would be looking for him soon, in a town of whose geography he was completely innocent. After all, he had been carried through the town unconscious. To deal with essentials only, he needed friends—and the only friend he had in Mexico was General Rafael Ortega. He cursed himself for forgetting to take his clothes along in the basket. But he could blame that on his fatigue.

Once more to essentials. Everyone else besides Ortega was willing to see him dead, including the wealthy but delicate *Señor* Gutierrez.

Therefore, he had no place else to go. He must find Ortega. Where was Ortega's last known position? At the scene of the ambush, Ortega had left the train on foot and had then melted into the countryside. He would go to the ambush site and then look for Ortega.

19

It began to rain from the dirty pewter-colored sky—a very cold and heavy rain. In a few minutes he was drenched through. He could see which way north was by the lightening of the sky to the east. He turned and headed in that direction.

After he got out of Torreón, he decided, he would have a clear view and would see the railroad tracks. If he happened to find himself in a valley, all he would do would be to climb a hill; then he would be able to spot the railroad immediately.

He plodded on, his *rebozo* over his head. He was hunched over in case he might run into someone who might catch sight of his bearded face. Around the next corner he bumped into a man wearing a poncho. The man was startled. His hand went under his poncho to his hip as he called out, "*Quien vive?* Who's there?"

The man wore a sugar-loaf hat and carried a Mauser. It was a *rurale*. Slocum gave a shrug, which expressed something like: Can't you see I'm a maid out shopping, you fool? The man did not stop him.

It was a close call. In a little while it would be too light for him to get away with this kind of a grotesque masquerade. He began to walk faster. The cold rain was increasing in intensity. His feet were so numb that they had lost all sensation. They felt like heavy logs attached to his ankles which he was condemned to drag through the puddles of icy rainwater and over the uneven cobblestones.

Luck was with him. At the next intersection he heard the solid *clang*! of two freight cars banging together, accompanied by the busy, self-important puffing of a yard engine making up a train. He swung in that direction. Five minutes later he stood on the outskirts of Torreón's railroad yards. The light had increased. It would be dangerous for him to meet anyone—it would be obvious to anyone that he was a man wearing women's clothes.

He padded along slowly, parallel to the rails. He was in luck: The train being made up was pointing to the north. A closer inspection showed that 12 units were empty ore cars; the rest of the 38-car train was comprised of cattle cars. Neither appealed to Slocum as a refuge from the rain, or from inquisitive *rurales*. The cattle cars were nothing but open-sided crates, the ore cars were simply long metal boxes, completely open at the top. A glance in each one by a *rurale* would immediately reveal Slocum's presence. The caboose was out of the question; there was always someone in it, either the conductor or the brakeman. Slocum moved across the tracks, taking small steps, so that at a distance, under the rapidly lightening sky, people might take him for a woman.

The cobblestones had been bad enough, but the cinders and gravel of the railroad yard were far worse. Slocum dared not pick his way carefully over that painful surface, in case he might be noticed doing so. No Indian woman with her calloused soles would do that. So he walked as if he were wearing boots, with no pains taken as to where he placed his bare feet.

He saw the engineer and fireman get off the locomotive in their raincoats. Good. They were going somewhere, and Slocum was sure, from his experience in railroading, that they were heading for a hot breakfast before they took their train north.

He decided his best course of action would be to move to the other side of the train and then move up to the locomotive, using the entire length of it as a cover till he reached the locomotive. In case the two men should happen to glance back, they would notice nothing, because he would be on the other side. What he wanted right then was to be near a locomotive's firebox. He was trembling uncontrollably from the cold.

He stepped on a rail and took a step that brought him between two of the ore cars which had a two-foot gap between them. At that split-second the little yard engine added another cattle car to the train. Only by a frantic spurt did Slocum escape being crushed as the two parts of the train locked together. As it was, his skirt was pinched tightly inside the coupling. He managed to free himself only by ripping the fabric loose. Even in the chilly, rain-soaked air he began to sweat.

"That was close," he said aloud in English. "*Jesus Christ Almighty!*"

He caught himself, realizing he could not afford the luxury of cursing aloud in his native tongue. Still sweating, he moved along the train. It was almost full light by now. He lifted a leg to the bottom rung of the ladder leading up to the cab and discovered what women have always known: The skirt had to be hoisted first. Once in the cab, he moved in front of the firebox. Heat radiated from it. He stood in front of it as long as he dared: five minutes. Feeling much better, he turned to the coal tender. It had just been filled, and there was loose coal on the floor plates of the cab. Good. The fireman wouldn't get near the back of the tender for hours yet.

Slocum clambered up to the top of the coal. When he reached the back of it, he carefully dug out a hole with his hands. He tried to pile up the coal he had removed so that he would be able to heap it around him once he was squatting down in the bottom, but a lot of the chunks rolled down and scattered across the floor of the cab. There was nothing he could do about that. He hoped it would not make either of the two men suspicious when they returned from their breakfast. He did the best he could. When he had finished, he heard horses' hooves clattering along the gravel and the jingle of their metal bits.

"*Que pasa?*" he heard a voice ask.

A crisp, arrogant voice demanded, "Is this your train, engineer?"

"*Sí, señor.*"

"We're searching for someone."

"Who?"

95

"A *gringo*."

"A what, *señor*?"

"*Cabrón!* A *gringo*, a *gringo*!"

"I have not seen any *gringos, señor*."

The patrol trotted down the length of the train. Slocum imagined what they were doing: Each man was rising in his stirrups each time they passed the ore cars to look inside, and as they rode beside the cattle cars they leaned forward to peer carefully in every corner. The clatter of the horses died down.

"*Maldita sea tu madre!*" muttered the engineer. "Cursed be your mother!" He turned to his fireman. "Diego, what's all this shit on the floor of the cab?"

"How the hell do I know?" replied the puzzled Diego. He angrily flung open the door to the firebox, and then Slocum heard the big, flat coal shovel scraping up the coal from the floorplates of the cab, and then the clang as the fire door was slammed shut. The train began to move. It crossed switchpoint after switchpoint as it moved through the yard and along the trackage. Slocum tensed; he knew he wouldn't really feel safe until the train cleared the yard and was moving at a fast clip outside of Torreón. Finally the train's wheels settled down to the steady *clackety-clack* of the main line track to the north. They were out of the yard at last.

A voice ahead yelled "Stop!"

"*Tu madre puta!*" muttered the engineer, enraged. He braked the train.

"Lieutenant Sandoval," the voice said in the tone of one used to command. "I must search this train."

"Someone just searched it!" shouted the engineer.

"And we will search it again," said Lieutenant Sandoval in great good humor. "You will not move it until I say you can. *Claro?*"

"*Sí, señor.*"

Once more Slocum listened to the horses' hooves

96

crunching along the gravel as the patrol divided in half, and each side of the train was carefully scrutinized.

"This *gachupin* is smarter than the other one," said the engineer. "The other one just walked along one side. This one is looking at both sides at once. Some day he will be a general."

"This must be an important *gringo*," said Diego, impressed. They began talking about their women. Slocum listened patiently, grateful for the warmth that flowed back from the firebox and for heading north at no expense to him. He heard the horses coming back.

"*Anda, anda!*" shouted the lieutenant.

The engineer shoved the throttle forward. "What did this *gringo* do?" he asked.

"What did he do?" repeated the officer. "My friend, I will tell you. To no one else will I tell this, but only to you."

"Yes?" said the engineer, flattered. He leaned out of the cab, cupping a hand behind his ear, as the lieutenant trotted beside the train.

"He let out a fart in Chapultepec Castle," said Lieutenant Sandoval gravely, while his men shouted with laughter.

20

Slocum had made himself a hollow in the coal so that the surrounding ring was higher than his head. The jiggle and bounce of the train ground out coal dust from the mass surrounding him and there was no way to avoid breathing it except to filter it through his *rebozo*. Now that the sun had risen, he was beginning to warm up. The numbness had left his feet and he was beginning to feel severe pain. Besides, he had cut his feet badly on broken glass as he walked through the yard, and now, as

97

the feeling returned to his feet, he became aware of that. One of the cuts was deep enough to worry him. The blood refused to coagulate, and he could feel it trickling out.

He dared not make any move to bandage it, lest he dislodge the coal and attract attention. He was also becoming thirsty. As the sun rose higher, it began to pound its force directly onto his head. He pulled part of the *rebozo* atop his bare head. Sunstroke was another burden, and he should avoid that, at least.

For a long time nothing happened except the occasional sounds of the fireman at work, the shrill scream of the whistle at crossings, and once again, the scraping sound of the flat shovel as it slid into the base of the coal in the tender, and then the clang of the furnace door as it opened and closed.

Suddenly the train jolted to a halt.

"Son of a bitch, prick, bastard!"

Then, after this passage of curses from the engineer, Slocum heard him ask in an angry manner, "What now?"

"Orders. We're searching the train."

"But it was searched twice in Torreón!"

"Telegraph orders from Colonel Escalante are to search your train. I search."

"But——"

"Shut up. Don't move it till I tell you to, or I'll cut off your balls and shove them up your asshole. Understand? *Adelante!*"

Under his breath Slocum heard the engineer whisper, "Miserable son of a whore! *Gachupin* prick!"

Again the sound of a patrol dividing in half, each half trotting alongside its side of the train. Then he heard the horses coming back. But instead of the cursory dismissal by the officer that Slocum had been expecting, Slocum heard the creaking of saddles as the officer and a sergeant dismounted and climbed into the cab.

"You think someone is in the firebox?" demanded the engineer, his voice heavy with resentment.

"These are a new pair of French kid gloves," the officer said. "They've been ruined by your filthy locomotive. Don't you ever wipe those railings? Sergeant, poke your bayonet in the coal."

Slocum tensed. He doubled his fists. He would have to explode out of there like a partridge out of its cover when the time came. He heard the grating sounds of the bayonet prying here and there, going in and out of the coal. He braced himself. Then the engineer, goaded beyond endurance, spoke.

The last remark of the officer about the dirty railings had been too much for his patience. "What the hell do you think this is, *cabrón*, the kitchen of Díaz?"

There was dead silence. The sergeant, shocked by the insult to his captain, stood paralyzed.

"What did you say?" demanded the officer quietly.

The engineer realized he had gone too far. Facing two armed soldiers in the cab—with 18 more just outside the cab, all armed and quite ready to kill him at a nod from their lieutenant—made the odds too heavy.

"I beg your pardon, *señor*. I was too excited."

"Ah," said the officer, relenting. The sergeant, staring at the engineer, made some halfhearted stabs at the coal.

"Sergeant?"

"Nada, mi capitán."

"Vamonos."

Slocum heard them climbing down. Then the sound of leather creaking as the two men swung into their saddles. Then there followed the sound of the patrol riding away.

"You were stupid," said the fireman.

"Hombre, do you blame me?"

"No. But it was very close, too close."

"Sí. I'd like to tear off that *gringo's* balls! It's all his fault."

Slocum bore him no resentment. After all, the engineer's vile temper had saved his life.

Two hours passed. The heat from the firebox, added to the vertical hammer blows from the sun overhead, increased Slocum's thirst to the point where he knew he might do something foolish just to a get a drink. Men dying of thirst perform ridiculous acts, he knew.

The train jerked once more to a halt. Another search? But this time the train went into reverse, clicked over a switchpoint, and halted. By the yelling back and forth between the brakeman and the engineer, Slocum knew that seven cattle cars were being dropped off at a siding. In five minutes, the job was done. Then Slocum heard the brakeman call out, "*Una bebida?* A drink?"

"Why not?"

The engineer and the fireman climbed down on the right side. Slowly and carefully Slocum emerged from his hollow. There was no one in the cab. He moved as quietly as possible to the bottom of the pile. He saw a canteen stuck under the fireman's seat. He picked it up. The sloshing noise inside told him what he wanted to know more than anything else in the world right then. He unscrewed the cap and drank it all. It was only a pint of warm water, but it was enough for him to feel enormously better. The canteen replaced, he peered cautiously over the side of the cab. The country was flat and covered with dusty *chaparral*. In the distance to the west was the blue-black mass of the Sierra Madre. He risked a quick look to the other side of the cab. He saw corrals and dust, and heard bawling cattle. He turned and climbed down the ladder on the west side. His feet hurt badly. At the last moment, just as he was about to relinquish his grip on the railings, he saw that he had left a series of bloody, smeared footprints leading from the coal tender to the ladder. He climbed back and wiped the floor clean with his *rebozo*. This time he crawled to the ladder, deliberately keeping his bleeding soles from the floor, and went down.

There was nowhere to hide. It would be best to stay in the train as long as he could for the cover it would provide. He saw a burlap sack lying by the track. He picked it up, walked to an ore car, climbed it, and slid down into the bottom. The metal was unbearably hot. He pulled off the *rebozo*, and, sitting on it for protection against the hot metal, started to unravel the burlap. The train began to move. In the next hour he had succeeded in making two burlap sandals. That done, he replaced the *rebozo* on his head and around his sunburned shoulders and back, and, sitting on what was left of the burlap, waited. The blood oozed from his torn feet but slowly began to coagulate, now that there was some protection. He waited. The sun moved slowly from the zenith and began to incline toward the west. Then the train began to slow down until its speed had dropped to ten miles per hour, as Slocum judged.

He heard his own engine coming closer, and he realized that they were on some sort of a switchback curve, almost like a hairpin in shape. He risked a careful peek. They were at the same horseshoe curve where he had been ambushed! This was perfect. It was time to leave, for if he wanted to find Ortega again, this was the best possible place to start looking. It was broad daylight, but this was a risk which had to be run. Slocum hoisted himself to the rim of the ore truck, clambered down as far as he could go, and, poising himself for a second, took a deep breath and let go.

The speed was still too much for Slocum's crippled feet. They could not take the strain. He fell and rolled over twice, scraping his torso and sunburned shoulders against the gravel. He rolled once more, into the *chaparral*, where he lay unmoving, hoping the conductor and brakeman would not be looking out of the caboose as it passed by. He swore silently at the various painful sensations he felt all over his body. He did not move until the sound of the engine had become faint in the distance.

A great burden was lifted from him. He felt like singing. Instead, he found himself laughing. When the laughter became too loud and uncontrollable, he realized he was verging upon hysteria. He told himself to shut up. He knew he had been very, very lucky to get away with his life, although he had suffered some painful but minor injuries, and the loss of some gold coins was, after all, a fair exchange. But he was stubborn. He wanted that money back. Not necessarily the exact gold coins stolen from him, by one of Escalante's men, when he was unconscious. Slocum would accept the equivalent in Mexican silver *pesos*, gold dust, or cattle. That was his minimal demand upon the citizenry of Mexico, and he didn't care whether the donor would be the army, various bandits, ranchers, or mine owners. He had only one restriction—the money would come from someone whose ethical standards he did not approve of.

But his first step would be to find Ortega. He did not blame the general for his situation, nor did he blame Ortega's probable inability to pay off on Slocum's investment—after all, that was due to the gods of war. His sole aim right then was to find Ortega, for he knew there he could at least find security and shelter.

Where would Ortega be? Slocum put himself in the man's place. Where would he go after such a stunning defeat? No rifles, no men, no supplies, no money. And with a large body of enemy soldiers chasing him? "Why," said Slocum aloud, "I'd go where horses would have a bad time, where a man could be seen a long way off, where hiding places and water would be everywhere, where two or three men could make a stand against an army."

And that meant the Sierra Madre. Slocum stood up and began walking toward the blue mass in the west. After two miles he reached a small pond covered with green scum. He knelt and brushed it aside. The water underneath was dark brown and it stank of cattle urine. Slocum bent down and drank it. He had tasted worse in his life. At least it was not poisonous. He had nothing to carry it in for future thirst. He cursed softly: He should have taken the fireman's canteen. But then, he realized, had he done so, the fireman would have guessed that the *gringo* was on the train. Slocum decided it was a good thing that he hadn't taken it. He soaked his *rebozo* in the pond and covered his head and shoulders with it. The damp cloth felt good against the constant burning sensation of his badly sunburned back and shoulders. At least it would protect him until the water evaporated.

He walked west across the stony soil, weaving in and out of the *chaparral*, but holding to a general westerly course. Rabbits panted under the shade of the bushes. Slocum found a strong dead branch and tried a few times to kill an occasional rabbit, but the creatures were too wary and fast for him.

The ground was covered with small pebbles and sharp little stones. He had never really noticed the harsh surface in those days when he rode horseback, or wore boots to protect his feet when he was afoot. The cuts in the soles of his feet opened up again under the strain, and he began leaving a bloody trail across the dusty desert surface.

He plodded grimly on. He found some *mesquite* and ate the ripened beans from the long, slender pods. It helped somewhat, but it made him thirsty again. He pulled up a corner of the *rebozo* and chewed on it. Enough moisture still remained in it to dampen his mouth.

The *chaparral* everywhere had a solidly woven texture, mostly gray, for the rains up here were still two months off. The sun flared overhead; it seemed to sear Slocum's exposed skin. He slowed and came to a stop. It would be far more intelligent for him to find a shady place and rest until dusk, no matter how thirsty he was. He was losing water too fast by the evaporation through his skin. He had no way of replacing it. He found a clump of *mesquite*. He pulled off his *rebozo* and spread it across some branches. It made a thin strip of shade, under which he crouched, moving with the shade as it angled to the east. He thought with a grim smile that he was emulating the panting rabbits he had seen. Then he occupied his mind with thoughts of what he would like to do to Escalante should they ever meet again.

This was not a profitable pursuit, however. Slocum was not given to childish daydreams of vengeance. He abandoned that sort of thinking and settled upon a much more intelligent course of thought: planning exactly how he would extract his money from Mexico. By the time it was cool enough to move, he had struck upon an idea which seemed workable, foolproof, and not expensive. It would take quick thinking, courage, and acting ability, but Slocum had enough of these. As he limped westward in the darkening air, he subjected his scheme to a heavy critical attack. But he could find no flaws in it. *None.*

22

The *rebozo* and the thin skirt were not effective in keeping him warm. He walked till he was exhausted. Then he sat down and slept a few minutes until the cold awakened him. He got up and moved again. He kept moving till dawn. He was utterly worn out. His feet were bleeding badly. He was famished and thirsty. If he had met a rabbit and killed it, he would have drunk its blood and eaten it raw. His back and shoulders had erupted in huge blisters.

At nine that evening he stumbled into a small Indian village in the foothills. The men of the village moved silently around him until they formed a ring of observers. They all carried machetes. Slocum did not have any idea how he appeared to these peasants, and he did not understand why they had removed their *sombreros* and crossed themselves as they stared at him in the light of their flickering torches.

What they saw was a tall figure with a five-day growth of black beard, black hair matted with coal dust and sweat, and bloodshot eyes staring out of a thin, drawn face smeared with coal dust. The upper torso was smeared black, but with white streaks left by little rivulets of sweat. There were large white blisters on his back and shoulders, either smeared with coal dust or burst open and suppurating from the red raw surfaces where the sweat had washed away the dust. They saw a horribly dirty skirt which had once been white, bare hairy legs sunburned and filthy with coal dust and sweat, and on the bottom of this amazing creature, the grotesque masses of burlap encasing his feet.

Of course the Indians thought he was a madman. They saw he was exhausted and hurt. A woman came to him and took his hand. He followed her into a hut. She gave him a clay jar filled with goat milk. He sipped it slowly in a kind of ecstasy. She took him by the arm and helped him limp to the back of the huts, where a cool, clear stream flowed over flat rocks in the shadow of giant ahuehuetes. The men silently surrounded them. She stripped Slocum of the skirt and the burlap sandals. The moon was almost full. He sat on the flat stones. The water came up to his waist. She scrubbed him with a rough, stinging laundry soap till he was clean. She took him back naked to the hut, made him lie down, and, with a bowl of water in which she had steeped some strange leaves, she gently washed his cuts and bruises.

Slocum felt unbearably sleepy. All he said, before he dropped off to sleep, was "Ortega. *Por favor.* General Ortega." Then he fell into the great, calm pool of sleep.

He slept 12 hours. When he woke, sunlight was streaming in through the front door of the hut. They gave him turkey and cold water from the clay pot. When he had eaten enough, he went to sleep again. When he opened his eyes five hours later, he saw Ortega grinning down at him.

23

"*Oye, gringo! Como 'sta?*"

"All right. And you?"

"Not so good. Not so good." He sighed and sat cross-legged beside Slocum. Ortega was wearing the white cotton peon pants and shirt of the area. He wore sandals, carried a machete, and wore a straw *sombrero*, as did everyone else around him. He looked just like a peon as long as he did not walk with his usual arrogant swagger.

106

"I have a few men now," Ortega said. "Maybe fifty, sixty." He looked around at the old woman behind him. She was silently pounding more leaves to make a poultice for Slocum's wounds. He grinned at her. She did not respond. "I see you have no clothes," Ortega went on. "I sent Luis for some. He will be back soon. They say you were dressed like a woman."

Slocum shrugged. "I got here," he said simply.

"I, too. And Luis. How did you know I was nearby?"

"I didn't. I thought you'd be hiding in the mountains, planning your next move while you did some recruiting. So I headed this way."

"Oh, you're very smart for a *gringo*," Ortega said admiringly. "You don't look so good. Your throat, especially. Who did it, that bastard Escalante?"

"Yes. I'll meet him again. How did you get away?"

Ortega grinned. "They never thought that Ortega and Arango would be in the locomotive! That's where workingmen belong, no? And since the tracks were blown at both ends of the train, why bother with the poor engineer and fireman, who were probably captured by Ortega, and only wanted to escape back into federal hands? Eh?" He chuckled. "So when we ran toward the *chaparral* they did not stop us. Here's Luis. Put the clothes on fast. It's too dangerous here, here in the flat country. The hills are too small around here, anyway. Besides, we are not well-liked."

Arango had tossed the clothes beside Slocum. Slocum nodded to Arango, who responded grudgingly. Not well-liked is right, Slocum thought.

Slocum dressed. He had the same peon clothes that everyone else was wearing. The cotton was heavy, but clean. The cuts on his feet were beginning to heal. It felt good to put on sandals. He felt incredibly light-footed after having worn the burlap monstrosities, and he enjoyed the thought that his feet wouldn't be cut or bruised anymore. There were several faces peering inside through the cracks in the crudely built hut.

One of them said gravely, "*Como va el loco?* How is the crazy man?"

"*'sta bien, 'sta bien,*" Ortega said genially. "We're taking him with us." An expression of relief flitted across the man's face. "We need corn and meat," Ortega said. The face became impassive. "And the same as before," Ortega added. No one moved. Slocum immediately sensed the unfriendly attitude. Ortega lifted the bottom of his blouse and placed his hand on the butt of a Colt that was stuck into his pants top. "I will pay, of course."

The man nodded reluctantly.

"*Pronto, amigo mío,*" Arango said.

It was said in a conversational tone, and anyone who did not know Arango might have thought that the two men were having a calm discussion about the weather, for instance. But they obviously had had experience with Arango. These three words were all that was necessary. The peons moved quickly. In a few minutes, sacks of corn and strips of dried beef were ready.

"How much?" asked Ortega gravely. The elder, who had asked about Slocum, now stood in front of Ortega with his *sombrero* in one hand. He shrugged helplessly.

"Twenty *pesos?*" Ortega said. "Thirty? Let us say forty."

Slocum could not understand the look of helpless resentment. Thirty *pesos* was a fair price—why should the man object to forty? Were these people idiots?

Ortega removed a wad of paper money from his pocket. He peeled off four bills and handed them over. The man took them with reluctance. Of course, Slocum thought, *now* I understand. Peons don't like paper money; it moulds, it rots, it can't be buried underground, the natural bank for people who don't trust banks. Mice

108

nibble on it, rats eat it or chew it up for their nests. No wonder he didn't want it; no wonder he preferred silver *pesos*. Still, if there was nothing else. . . . Peasant fools, Slocum thought.

The supplies were slung on a mule. They mounted the three other mules, which were nibbling intently at the cactus fence around a garden and rode off. The people were strangely quiet in the village. There was something eerie about the situation, and it gave Slocum an unpleasant sensation. His back tensed, as if it expected a machete slash to be delivered to it by one of the peons as Slocum rode by on his mule. Ortega did not look behind once, but rode unconcernedly on.

When they were trotting briskly, Ortega dropped behind until he was beside Slocum.

"What did you think of them?" he asked idly.

"Idiots."

"No," Ortega said. "Eminently sensible." He peeled off a ten-*peso* note and handed it to Slocum. It looked just like the regular Díaz note, but instead of Díaz's stern, heavily mustached portrait, this bill boasted an engraving of Ortega in a general's uniform, and under his portrait were the words INDEPENDENCE, LAND, FREEDOM in an elaborate scrollwork.

"I see you looked ahead," Slocum remarked.

"Yes. I had them printed up for me secretly in California. There were three packing cases of these notes aboard our train. I had a roll of them in my pocket when we were ambushed. The bastards burned them and what they didn't burn they used for toilet paper."

"And when the peons went to town with them they received a rude reception."

"*Sí*," Ortega grinned.

"Why don't they just refuse to sell you anything except for silver?"

"Ah," Ortega said, patting his gun butt. "There is no

109

silver, of course. And then I tell them we have thirty, forty men living in the caves up in the mountains. So when we come down for supplies, they sell it to us, even for this paper. This is the second time I have come in four days."

"How many men do you have?"

"None," said Ortega. A wide grin spread across his face. "We take supplies for thirty men in order to persuade them to be kind to us."

"Why don't they send someone up to the mountains to see how many there really are?"

"I thought this would occur to them," answered Ortega, "so I casually made the remark that I have several men—who have the bad habit of killing all strangers—watching the approaches."

"You would be a very good poker player," Slocum said.

"I have heard much of this game, *señor*. I would appreciate learning it. We will have much time till I put another army together. You are welcome to stay with me as long as you wish."

"Con mucho gusto."

But Slocum had opposite views on this matter. He decided to wait till everyone had eaten and rested before he sprung his scheme. There would be no time available to teach Ortega the game of poker in the leisurely manner the Mexican envisaged.

24

After a supper of *tortillas,* chicken, and *pulque*—which was prepared by Arango in his usual sullen fashion—Ortega and Slocum wrapped blankets around themselves and sat at the lip of the cave. The cave opened onto a *barranca*, at the bottom of which foamed a narrow, violent green river.

A vast, jumbled range, without any visible pattern of order, spread out before them, glowing pink in the setting sun. Slocum heard faint bird cries, but aside from that, there was no sound except the wind and the river's rumble far below.

"What are your plans?" asked Slocum. He was enjoying his first cigarette in days.

"In a month, maybe two," Ortega answered, "Díaz will stop sending out patrols. Then I'll build another army. And you will be useful to me, *señor*. I will need guns and ammunition. You will be the perfect man to buy them for me. Then——"

"No."

Ortega frowned. Arango lifted his head at hearing his general thus calmly defied. "*Señor?*" Ortega asked politely.

"No," Slocum repeated. "It won't work. You can't build an army by making the people hostile. You might recruit bandits, but you are not going to go anywhere with such an army. Others will offer them better pay and uniforms, and sooner or later they will betray you and hand you over to Díaz. No."

Ortega poked a stick angrily at the fire.

"And sooner or later," Slocum went on remorselessly, "one of the peons below there will slip into town and tell the commander of *rurales* where you are. They will seal all the passes. It will be hard to be lucky twice."

Ortega brooded.

"You need money," Slocum continued. "With money you can leave the country and be safe while you slowly and carefully build an army, paying for everything. No looting. Thus you will have a loyal peasantry; thus you will recruit from among them."

111

"You are telling us very important news," Arango burst out angrily from inside the cave. "We need *money*! *That* is amazing news. I wonder why *we* never thought of it?"

"*I* can get you the money," Slocum said calmly, disregarding Arango's outburst.

"Why do you want to help us?" demanded Arango suspiciously. There was a reward out for Ortega and Arango, Slocum knew, and Arango never trusted anyone's good will.

"Because you owe me a lot of money," Slocum said patiently. "I want it. Besides, I would like a word or two with Colonel Escalante. And this way I am pretty sure he'd be talking to me."

"How do I get this money?" Ortega asked.

"Ah," said Slocum.

25

The first step of Slocum's plan called for him to go to Laredo and outfit himself to look like an American mining engineer. That and later steps would cost about 500 dollars. But no one had any money. How could he get it?

Ortega liked Slocum's scheme immediately. He had the answer. He pointed out that they had plenty of supplies. It would not be hard for them to make their way to Tamaulipas in ten days or so, without being forced to enter any town. Once in ranch country in the north, they could quietly—with the ranchers unconscious of the trade—exchange their mules for horses. With the horses they would then collect about 30 decent head of cattle. Even 40. A discreet crossing of the Rio Grande and Slocum would sell them, pretending to be a cattle dealer temporarily strapped for immediate cash. Thus, they would then possess the necessary capital, without arousing the countryside—which is what would happen if they robbed a bank.

It was a good plan; even Arango assented grumpily to it. They proceeded to carry it out immediately, leaving before sunrise. By 11:00 they had climbed to the opposite ridge, completely unseen. They observed with great interest the careful stalking of their just-vacated cave by several troops of *rurales*. They moved quickly along the narrow mountain trails, sticking to rock surfaces, on their sure-footed mules. Mules would do better and move faster on such surfaces than horses.

"See," Ortega said, grinning, "we have been lucky twice. And, I must admit, this time we owe it to you, *señor*."

The *rurales* could not find their trail on rock. Four days later their route took them close to the roadside statue of the Virgin, to whom they had made their offerings—was it only two weeks ago? It was hard to believe that so much had happened in so short a time. Arango stared at her. A curious glittering expression filled his brown eyes in his hard bronze face. He stood in his stirrups, reached out, and wrenched the Virgin loose. He tossed her onto the ground.

"Whore!" he said succinctly.

They rode on in silence.

A good mule in mountain country was always worth more than a horse. They were sure-footed, never got nervous on heights, and ate nothing. It was easy to trade the mules in Saltillo for decent horses, and for enough *pesos* to buy second-hand boots and spurs. In two days they had found an isolated grassy valley where they saw a few hundred head of cattle grazing placidly. They cut out 30 of the best two- and three-year-old steers. Arango wanted to take more. Slocum pointed out that 30 would be plenty to handle for three men moving as fast as they

113

could, particularly since they would have no time to break the cattle to trail movement.

The next night they reached the river and swam the cattle across. Slocum immediately rode into Laredo. He found a dealer at the stockyards next morning. The man rode out and paid 40 dollars cash per head, no questions asked. He bought their horses for 60 dollars each—pleased to do so, since he so seldom handled any with Arab blood.

Slocum gave 100 dollars each to Ortega and Arango and rehearsed once more everyone's role in their elaborate scheme. Satisfied, he shook hands. They had enough money to live on until he would show up at the rendezvous. They took the next train to Monterrey, looking exactly like Mexican *vaqueros* who had gone up to the States with a load of cattle, seen what it was like, and were returning to their ranch with a little money actually left over.

After they had left, Slocum bought a good suit of clothes, as would befit a successful mining engineer. He bought good boots and an expensive Stetson—all secondhand, so that reasonable signs of wear would show. He dropped in at a printer's and purchased cards engraved with the following:

ALEXANDER GARRISON
Mining Engineer and Consultant
824 Post Street
San Francisco, California

It amused him to use the same initials in his phony name as those of Aurelio Gutierrez, who would soon have cause to hate this particular card. He next wrote a letter to a lawyer friend who could be trusted to keep his mouth shut. After reading the letter, the lawyer would see to it that the words on the card would be immediately transferred to his door in gold leaf. If any questions were asked in the next two weeks or so, Slocum asked, would the lawyer be good enough to answer frankly that Mr. Garrison had rented office space there for several years, was most reliable, and paid his rent promptly?

He next bought a good but battered second-hand suitcase. He filled it with second-hand boots, for working in the field, worn pants, for the same, two worn shirts, underwear, and socks. He then placed inside the suitcase a transit book, plenty of pencils, a second-hand theodolite he had picked up in a hockshop, and a copy of *Refining Precious Metal Wastes*, which he had found in the stationery shop where he had purchased his pencils and the transit book. All these were important, because he confidently expected that someone down in Mexico would be poking around in the suitcase, with deeply interested curiosity.

When he walked down the sidewalk, he looked exactly like a hard-bitten mining engineer with plenty of experience under his belt, even to the bulge on his hip where a plain, serviceable Colt was resting.

He picked up the cards and placed five of them in a worn card case, which he had found in the same hockshop where he had bought the theodolite. The dealer threw it in free. Slocum discreetly burned the other 995 cards. Then he walked to the depot and bought a ticket for Torreón.

26

He stepped off the train a day and a half later. He had slept well. He had shaved. In the three weeks which had gone by since he had escaped from Torreón, he had developed a thick mustache which completely changed his appearance. It made him seem far older. He had asked a barber to dye his hair and mustache here and there with

115

gray, and this reinforced the overall look of late middle-age that he wanted. He now had the appearance of a man 15 years older. He had had his hair neatly trimmed in Laredo. He figured he was a far cry in appearance from the dirty, bedraggled, messed-up prisoner, drawn and exhausted from hunger, thirst, and lack of sleep, whom Escalante and Gutierrez had looked at three weeks before.

And life had shown Slocum the truth of the old proverb "Clothes make the man." People *did* look at one's clothes more than one's face; that was how most people made their judgments on whether they should talk with a man or simply disregard him. Also, the expression was important. Slocum would have a calm, relaxed expression as he expounded his views and proposition—far, far unlike his pinched, angry, tortured expression as he was being heaved up by his neck by that rawhide *reata*. He had no doubt that he could get away with it.

Slocum set his suitcase down on the platform and slowly removed a good cigar from his pigskin-covered, metal-lined cigar case. That was another detail he was relying upon: the half-unconscious assumption the Mexicans would make—that no one who had been tortured in that house would ever use such a cigar case. And, of course, there would be still another assumption—why should anyone who had escaped with his life from that house deliberately come back and stick his head neatly in another noose? It was unlikely that they would even think it possible. In fact, it was unlikely that they would think about it.

Slocum struck a match, and as he lit his cigar, he surveyed Torreón with a great and judicious calm—as befit a mining engineer who was doing well.

It was a town like any other town, he decided. Typical were the massive stone facades, the elaborate carving

116

around the windows, and the thick iron grillwork over the windows. When open, the windows were still shielded from the view of passersby by wooden shutters. There was an occasional plaza with its thick groves of shade trees and flowering bushes, flower-bordered walks, comfortable benches, and a bandstand. The narrow streets were paved with cobblestones, and down the center ran channels made of gently sloping flagstones over which rainwater gushed during the occasional torrential downpours. This was the first time he was looking at it without great pressure to survive or depart. He had little affection for Torreón, to put it mildly. He picked out a coach from the several that thronged the station plaza clamoring for his trade. He asked for the second-best hotel—after all, a successful mining engineer would not be throwing away his money like a drunken cowboy on payday.

"*Posada del Norte*," recommended the coachman.

"*Vamonos.*"

It amused Slocum to notice several of the same streets he had padded down barefoot in flight. And to think he was now *riding* over them, leaning back in comfort and smoking a fine Havana! He shook his head in silent amusement. Things like this made life worth living. He laughed aloud.

"*Señor?*"

"*Cochero!*"

"*Sí, señor?*"

"Where is the house of *Don* Aurelio Gutierrez?"

"Three blocks that way, *señor*. That house brings honor to Torreón, *señor*."

"Please drive past it."

"*Con mucho gusto.*"

The horse clip-clopped by the house. And there it was, the same gates, the same vicious shards of glass set atop the wall. Then, as Slocum and the *cochero* moved past

117

the gate, he caught a fast glimpse of the lush green foliage and the water splashing in the two fountains— the same water that Colonel Escalante would not let him drink. There were no soldiers visible either at the gate nor inside. Good. Escalante would be out busily chasing Ortega somewhere far to the north—together with the French lady, who by now had probably found the colonel able to function horizontally.

Slocum told himself he would catch up with Escalante some day. It would not be hard to track him down in Mexico. Separated paths sometimes came together in amazing ways. Slocum promised himself he would be ready for that moment when it came.

There were only two people to take care of in Mexico: Escalante and Arango. He sighed and drew on his cigar. In one corner of the garden, just as the coach was about to turn the corner, he saw a head, covered with a black lace mantilla, bending over embroidery. *Don* Aurelio's wife had finally returned from Paris. She must have been thoroughly scandalized to learn what had happened in her best bed while she was away. Slocum grinned as he thought of the gossip he had picked up as he lay inside that house, trussed up like a Christmas goose. It would be amusing to enter it again—which was why he had come to Torreón.

27

After he had changed to a fresh shirt, had shaved again, and had his boots polished till they glowed, he hired another coach and ordered the *cochero* to drive to the Gutierrez house. The *cochero* banged on the gate and when a frightened Indian servant came, he gave her Slocum's business card and brusquely ordered her to tell

118

Don Aurelio that an important North American was waiting. The girl trotted off, vastly impressed, holding the card by a corner between her thumb and forefinger as if it were a piece of delicate and fragile porcelain.

She was back in a minute.

"*Don* Aurelio says please come in, *señor*," she said, staring with wide eyes at Slocum who, now that he was well-dressed and well-fed, was a handsome and imposing figure. A manservant now came and unlocked the gate and swung it open. Slocum entered and followed her, looking about him with the idle curiosity of a man who had never been there before. He walked along one side of the *patio*, past the tubs filled with huge pink oleanders in full bloom. Other tubs were filled with white camellia plants; Slocum particularly admired the brilliant green foliage set off against the pure, creamy white of the petals. He walked into the entrance hall, never forgetting to glance with admiration at the carved wooden statues and the paintings. From the hall he was escorted to a great room with a great fireplace. On one wall was a life-size oil portrait of a man in the eighteenth-century costume of a viceroy. Across the room was a four-foot-tall crudely carved wooden statue of Saint James on horseback, holding aloft a sword.

The girl giggled and withdrew, her bare feet slapping the tile floor. The sun poured vertical slats of golden light through the shutters, closed against the powerful afternoon sun. It was very quiet. Somewhere in the house there was a faint clatter of crockery and laughter; the kitchen help was preparing dinner. Slocum was too restless to sit in the overstuffed armchair with its mahogany armrests and its antimacassar, probably crocheted by *Señora* Gutierrez as she sat in the *patio*, afternoon after afternoon. He stood up and began to pace back and forth, remembering what had happened to him in this

119

house with the full consent of its owner. He hoped he would be able to control himself when he came face to face with *Don* Aurelio.

"*Señor* Garrison?"

Slocum composed his face, turned to face Gutierrez, and spoke in an amiable manner. "Yes, *señor*. I have called on a matter of business."

"You are from the United States?"

"Yes, *señor*."

"But you speak excellent Spanish!"

"Thank you. I have worked as a mining engineer in Peru and Colombia for many years."

Slocum had picked those two countries because it would take too long for Gutierrez to do any careful checking so far away. And Slocum also was careful to keep any Mexican phrases from his speech.

"I see. But before we discuss what is on your mind, please sit down! My manners are very poor. Brandy? Beer?"

"Brandy."

Don Aurelio opened a walnut cabinet and took out the same cut-glass decanter that Slocum had last seen in Escalante's hands. *Don* Aurelio removed two brandy snifters from the cabinet and poured. Slocum swished his brandy around and around his glass. Memories flooded him.

"A rare bouquet, no?"

"Without doubt, *señor*."

"My name is Aurelio. And you are—Alexander, I see. Why, *señor*, we have the same initials! *Don* Alejandro, without even knowing why you are here, I drink to your health!"

Slocum smiled. *Don* Aurelio was drinking to his health, yet not long ago he had donated the house to a man who was devoting himself to destroying that same health. Life could be very funny.

"And to yours, *Don* Aurelio."

Slocum knew the obligatory 20-minute period of polite, noncommittal conversation: weather, crops, politics, women, children. All these topics had to be gone through before the real business of the afternoon could be mentioned.

Finally Gutierrez asked mildly, "And what, *Don* Alejandro, brings you to Torreón?"

"It is very simple, *Don* Aurelio. I have discovered that there is more money to be made mining the less-valuable metals than in the valuable ones."

"Interesting. But I am not quite sure what you mean."

"I will be specific. Although gold and silver do attract more money for investment, very frequently the simpler elements produce more money."

Gutierrez was very interested, as Slocum knew he would be. Any investor in the broad spectrum of Mexican products, as Gutierrez was, was bound to be interested in what Slocum had just said so casually.

"Go on, *señor*."

"One reason, of course, is that gold and silver are usually never found in a pure state anymore. Most of the alluvial gold has been picked up. Now they occur as ores."

Gutierrez sighed and nodded knowingly. "Yes," he said gloomily.

Good, Slocum thought. The man has made bad investments in gold; he will listen even more carefully.

"And ores," Slocum went on, "have to be crushed. That takes very expensive machinery. Water is necessary. That can be a serious problem. Expensive chemicals are necessary in order to amalgamate whatever gold traces there are. Then expensive railroads have to be built to haul the ore. That means bridges. Shafts have to be dug and stopes. That means timber has to be brought enormous distances. It means sawmills. I do not even men-

121

tion the constant threat of robbery. Result: more money for armed guards. Another hidden cost: the permanent tension under which the supervisory staff—not to mention the investors—live."

"You have put it very well, *señor*. You have found a very profitable gold mine with very rich ore requiring very little treatment and—however, some capital?"

"No, *Don* Aurelio," Slocum said smiling. "Permit me. Salt mines are very, *very* profitable. One digs it up. That's all there is to it. No one kills anyone to secure a load of salt. Dig it and sell it. The same is true of guano deposits. Dig it with a shovel, put it in sacks—and you become rich."

"True. I understand your point. But why do you come to me, *señor*?"

"Because," said Slocum slowly, "I have just discovered the richest deposit of phosphorus I have ever seen in my life."

"But what——"

"And you own the match concession for Mexico."

Gutierrez's eyebrows went up. "Ah," he said thoughtfully.

Slocum was jubilant. He concealed his emotion. He likes the bait, Slocum thought. Now to persuade him to swallow it, hook and all.

"It is very close to a railroad. The spur track can be built very cheaply. I have looked over the contours—no bridges or grading will be necessary. It is close to a town, so you will have a large, cheap labor supply. You are close to water and close to wood."

"Why do you mention wood?"

"Because it could be a good idea, as long as you have the match concession, to make your own matches instead of importing them. Double your profit overnight."

Gutierrez sipped his brandy. Slocum could see the man was fascinated with the whole concept.

"Why pay someone to make matches? Why should he profit? Why pay shipping costs across the Atlantic?"

"Why, indeed?" murmured Gutierrez. It was clear to Slocum that the Mexican was quickly weighing the possibilities, one of which was, as Slocum well knew, a way to dump the *gringo* once the project was safely under way.

"Match-making machinery," Slocum went on, sinking the hook deeper," is very simple. If there is a breakdown, it can be very quickly repaired by mechanics who can be speedily trained for such work. If you mine your *own* phosphorus—and I've made a few test drillings in the area and estimate the deposit will yield sixty to eighty million tons of phosphoferrite, a very simple compound easily broken down to phosphorus in a simple, cheap operation—the savings and profit will be tremendous. Not only that, you will be able to undersell even the Swedish manufacturers you are buying from right now. You will be able to sell your own matches in *Sweden*—not to mention the United States and Canada."

Gutierrez let out a long, deep breath.

"And, if you don't care to invest your money, it will be easy to float your own stock shares, once several independent mining engineers make their own evaluation and report back to possible investors. You will control the shares, of course, and determine the dividends."

Gutierrez liked that, Slocum could see. *Don* Aurelio saw very quickly how easy it would be to milk the profits for his own pocket. I'm a thief, thought Slocum, but I take my chances. This thief cheats everyone and never suffers. Slocum sat in the comfortable chair, sipping his brandy and concealing his contempt for *Don* Aurelio.

"I don't know," Gutierrez said, pretending casualness. "There are just too many problems here. Where did you say this phosphorus is?"

"I did not say, *señor.*"

123

"Of course."

"*Don* Aurelio, let me be frank."

"Please."

"I know where the phosphoferrite is. No one else does. You have the money necessary to develop it. Neither of us can proceed without the other. Why not consider this at your leisure? I am staying at the Posada del Norte." Slocum stood up, carefully placing the brandy snifter on the table.

Gutierrez stood also. "My dear fellow," he said smoothly, "there is no need for you to stay in a hotel when I have such a big house. Juanito!"

"*Sí, Don* Aurelio."

A quiet little man of medium height entered the room. He gave Slocum a hard stare.

"*Señor* Gomez, *Señor* Garrison."

The two men murmured their greetings. Slocum's opinion of Gomez was that he was very hard, very shrewd, very careful.

"*Señor* Gomez is my accountant and general manager. I would like him to listen to your proposal—but only after dinner this evening. Juanito, would you be good enough to pick up *Señor* Garrison's luggage from the Posada del Norte?"

"*Sí, Don* Aurelio."

"With your permission, *Don* Alejandro." Gutierrez withdrew, taking Gomez by the elbow. Slocum sat down again with a contented smile. Gomez's function in fetching his luggage—which any *mozo* could do—was clear. He would open it and examine the contents. He would then report to Gutierrez. If it looked good, business would proceed at dinner. But it looked as if the bait had been swallowed all the way. Time would tell.

Gutierrez came in again.

"And now, *Don* Alejandro, may I show you to your

124

room? You must be tired. I will have hot water brought for your bath. You may like a nap before dinner. *Señora* Gutierrez will join us, and she is very demanding as to my guests' appearances. Afterwards, we can go over your proposal step by step."

"Enchanted."

Slocum rose. It would be a pleasure to get a decent meal and pass a restful night in this house, he thought, before Gutierrez stuck his head further into the noose which Slocum and Ortega were preparing for him.

Slocum slept well after his bath. A discreet tap at his door woke him.

The maid's voice said, "*Ya listo, Don* Alejandro."

Dinner was ready, then. Slocum shaved carefully. His shirt had been washed, dried and ironed. His trousers had been pressed. His underwear had been washed and ironed, and everything had been neatly laid out. A small metal chest stood on a table, and in it, resting on a cake of ice, were several bottles of the excellent Mexican beer.

For a moment Slocum daydreamed what Gutierrez's face would look like if he were to mention idly to his host just what his former food and accommodations had been like. It was a pleasure, alas, that he would have to postpone.

Slocum dressed, combed his hair, and walked down the corridor. At the head of the stairs, which were covered with yellow tiles arranged in a flower pattern, there screeched a magnificent yellow, green, and red macaw.

Gutierrez and Gomez were standing on the landing, waiting for him. "You have seen my macaw?" Gutierrez demanded. "It has come from the *tierra caliente*. I ordered it as a pet for my wife; such unusual things please her. I think it is the only one in Torreón." He stared up the stairs at the bird. "There are times when I

125

would like to twist its neck, but my wife has a fondness for the bird." It was clear that Gutierrez had a deep affection for his wife.

"You will have to learn how to live with it," Slocum said, descending the stairs.

"I seem to hear some dearly bought wisdom, *Don* Alejandro."

"No one knows what lurks in the heart of a woman. Least of all the lady herself."

Gutierrez clapped him on the back. "Look who we have here, Juanito! A *gringo* philosopher—*and* a mining engineer!"

"A very strong combination, to be sure," murmured Gomez. Slocum smiled at him amiably, but under his placid face he was trying to figure out how Gomez had made out with his luggage inspection. Everything had been replaced exactly where it had been before, so whoever had done it was very discreet, very intelligent, and possessed, as well, an excellent memory. A formidable opponent. And, if he knew his craft as a financial advisor, he had had time to stop off at the telegraph office and wire a reliable business contact in San Francisco to check out 824 Post Street.

But the general mood seemed to be excellent. The point was not to rush things. The answer from San Francisco wouldn't come till tomorrow. Therefore, Slocum decided, he would present his case in a leisurely manner, backing it up with some figures concerning phosphoferrite excavation costs, match-manufacturing machinery costs (here he would be making a wild guess, but by the time verification would come on that item Gutierrez would be heartily sick of the match business anyway), and similar matters.

Gutierrez wore very tight black trousers with old silver coins attached along the outside seams, and a white, ruffled shirt. "My wife likes these *ranchero* affairs," he said. "Eh, Juanito?"

Gomez produced a sour smile. He was plainly dressed, as befitted a financial advisor and accountant. It was clear to Slocum that Gomez did not care for the *señora*.

"And there she is!" said Gutierrez proudly.

Slocum removed his cigar and turned to greet *Señora* Gutierrez. But it was Ghislaine Marchand who advanced toward him, smiling.

28

Later Slocum would wonder how he had been able to keep his mouth from gaping open in astonishment. But he did it, and by the time Ghislaine had reached the group, his face expressed nothing but polite interest.

She wore the long, white embroidered peasant dress of Yucatán. Upper-class women in Mexico simply did not wear such things, preferring the latest Paris fashions. But Ghislaine, as Slocum had come to realize, did not care what society considered fashionable.

Her hair was coiled several times around her head in smaller and smaller concentric circles. It looked very much like a coiled snake, and at the very small summit of this mound there stood a gold comb set with two emeralds; the illusion of a snake's head was perfect. Slocum did not care for the resemblance. He noticed the faintest blue marks on her throat. He must have squeezed her harder than he thought.

"May I present my wife?" Gutierrez said proudly. "And, my dear, this is an American here on business—*Don* Alejandro Garrison."

Slocum bowed. He looked at her with the correct degree of polite interest mixed with admiration. His eyes, under his calm demeanor, looked hard for any sign whatsoever that she knew him. He saw none.

"*Encantado, señora.*"

"*Tampóco, señor.* I have heard about you." Her face, like his, expressed nothing but polite amiability. Was it possible she hadn't recognized him? She had never seen him shaven and well-groomed, after all. And what was all this about "*Señora* Gutierrez"? Had the real one died in Paris? Had he married Ghislaine? Or was she his mistress? After all, Gutierrez had far more money and led a safer life than all the generals or colonels she had been used to. Perhaps she had finally decided to move upwards socially?

"His name is Alejandro, my dear. Alejandro the Great! He has come to conquer us." From the corner of his eye Slocum saw Gomez's sour smile. If Gomez had anything to do with it, Slocum knew, Alexander would leave Mexico quite the reverse of a conqueror.

"Bad things happen to people who wish to conquer," she said with a thin sardonic smile.

"Not always, *señora.*"

"That is true. Shall we go in to dinner?" she said and took Slocum's arm.

Dinner was a calm affair. She discussed the opera she had attended in Mexico City four days ago, a novel by Balzac, and whether she should buy a Corot or two for the dining room. American literature was discussed, but Slocum politely declined to volunteer any information on that subject, mentioning that, unfortunately, he was too busy to do any reading except books on mining. The food was excellent, and the Indian maids padded silently around the table. Ghislaine had made no sign of recognition at all. Slocum was feeling relieved.

After dinner they moved to the drawing room. Gutierrez took Gomez's arm and whispered briefly. Gomez nodded and left, after a bow to Ghislaine and Slocum. He was off to pick up the answering telegram, Slocum was sure, just in case there had been an immediate response. The conversation after he left turned to trivia: weather, prices of cattle, the recent ambush of the rebel General Ortega outside of Torreón. They sipped their brandy and chatted. In 15 minutes, Gomez returned and handed Gutierrez a telegram. Gutierrez read it, smiled, and crumpled it. He turned with a relaxed smile to Slocum.

"*Don* Alejandro," he said with a friendly manner, "let us discuss specifics."

"Gladly."

"But I see no reason to talk business in front of *Señora* Gutierrez."

She rose. "It bores me, you see. But before you go, *Don* Alejandro, I'd like to show you where I plan to place my Corots."

"What Corots?" asked Gutierrez with a startled look.

"The ones I will buy in Paris next month, of course, *mi amor.*"

Slocum could see that this was the first time that Gutierrez knew that she was going to Paris to buy Corots. A worried look swept over his face. Slocum was sure that *Don* Aurelio was thinking: suppose the two women met? Ghislaine was a large bundle and had to be paid for in other things beside money.

"*Don* Alejandro," she said smiling and taking Slocum's arm, "do you like the idea I have of placing one of the Corots there, on the wall, near the fireplace? Or would it be better next to that window?"

"I'm afraid I don't know anything about paintings." She made him uneasy. He didn't trust her.

"Corot painted trees and meadows," she said. "The dominant color is always green. Or perhaps here would be better, next to the statue of Saint James? The brown

129

of the wood would set off the green nicely, don't you think?"

They were moving farther away from Gutierrez and Gomez, who were talking intently and not looking at them. They were no doubt, thought Slocum, deep in conversation about his credit references.

"Remember, *Don* Alejandro, there will be a great deal of *green*. I really do think that next to the statue would be best." Then she added, in exactly the same tone, "I'll come to your room about one in the morning. Do not lock your door. Perform well this time, or I'll tell Gutierrez who you are. Or do you think I should drop the idea of Corot entirely and concentrate on Millet? Millet is more colorful than Corot, you see, and, after all, don't you think that is precisely what this room needs?"

"Yes," Slocum said. What *he* really needed, in his sincere opinion, was to see her heartily slapped, left palm and right, all the way across that room and back. He would be happy to put his shoulders behind that effort.

But it wouldn't happen. His destiny that night would be to bring pleasure to the lady so that there'd be no complaints whatsoever. *None.* Or he'd be very dead by morning.

29

The business talk was intensely detailed. Slocum was calm and very convincing. There would be no need, he pointed out, for Gutierrez to invest a single cent until he was absolutely sure that the venture would be profitable. The essential point was that there be a vast and easily worked deposit of phosphoferrite. If there was, the rest of the matter would be purely automatic.

Slocum said casually that he had taken an option on the phosphorus area. Once Gutierrez was thoroughly convinced that the whole concept would be feasible, Slocum would then transfer the option to Gutierrez upon the latter's signing a contract giving Slocum five percent of the gross sales of the completed match factory. Since he needed money to live on during the two or three years it would take to start the mine and build the factory, he would want to be hired as the mining engineer and be paid separately on that basis. It was a very good deal for Gutierrez, and Slocum knew it. He could see Gutierrez's big smile when he listened to the terms, and heard the phrase, "transfer of option." Slocum understood that smile. The smile meant that lawyers and landowners would be involved; and that meant Mexican lawyers and Mexican landowners. And ultimately, a Mexican judge. And Gutierrez was a very good friend of Porfirio Díaz. And who appointed and controlled the judges? *Don Porfi.* Slocum knew that Gutierrez and Gomez fully intended to deliver one magnificent shafting and after all, why not? He was only a *gringo* and the phosphorus was Mexican.

"You look tired, *Don* Alejandro," Gutierrez said, rising. "I also. And——" here he looked upwards toward his bedroom and smiled—— "I have business to take care of." He bowed and left, followed by Gomez in that man's usual discreet and self-effacing manner. The maid padded in, picked up a kerosene lamp attached to a wall bracket, said softly, "*Señor?*" and waited. Slocum stood up and followed her through the great, stone-paved corridors, up the staircase, and along the hall till they reached his room. She opened the door, set the lamp on his table, and, thrusting a hand into her décolleté, withdrew a folded note. It read:

Lock your door with plenty of noise. But be sure the French window is left open. You and I have a contract which was unilaterally abrogated by you a few weeks ago. You understand why it would be best for you to fulfill it tonight. I shall come after he falls asleep—around one. I will come just after the church bells ring. Give this note back to the maid.

Slocum did so. The maid held it above the lamp until it flared up and burned to a crumpled black ash. All women are naturally shrewd and demanding in pursuing their one great interest, Slocum mused. The maid did not smile. Slocum opened the door for her. She padded out, her single long black braid tied with a length of scarlet wool, swaying down past her hips. Slocum banged the door shut behind her, following instructions, and turned the huge old key noisily in the lock. Then he rammed the big iron bolt home. Slocum guessed that the purpose of this noisy little performance was to reassure Gutierrez that this guest had no designs upon the maids' honor and that he was safely tucked away till morning.

He woke up to the ringing of the church bells. It was something he had never gotten used to, no matter how often he was in Mexico—the wild, discordant clamor of the bells, ringing in a haphazard manner all through the night. He turned toward the French windows. The big branches and the leaf canopy of the great ahuehuetes outside his balcony kept most of the moonlight out. He thought about Ghislaine. She was a beautiful woman— probably the most stunning that Slocum had ever seen. She was very much in demand among Mexico's more successful military and financial classes. She was very interested in him, and whereas most men would feel flattered about this, Slocum preferred to do his own hunting. For him the chase was exciting—especially if there was a chance of failure. For it was the ever-present possibility of failure that gave zest to the chase; if he were sure he would win each time, where was the suspense? This was the reason, for instance, why Slocum did not frequent whorehouses; if he could rent a woman by shelling out some money, there was no suspense.

But he had to be realistic. Suspense or not, he knew he had to satisfy the lady—or he would regret it. He could avoid that risk by dressing and making his way along one branch of the ahuehuete and then climbing down the trunk, but that would be the end of his Mexican investment for all time. He took a deep breath and decided to risk his life once more.

The moonlight was suddenly blotted out. Slocum slipped silently from his bed and moved to the foot of it, motionless. The moonlight resumed. Someone had come into the room. He didn't trust her. He considered her capable of killing him in his sleep; she might have reconsidered her feelings when he had failed her the first time and then strangled her into unconsciousness. He stood naked and immobile. She would have to make the first move.

She wore a long white silk dressing gown. Her long hair, like her Indian maid's, was braided together in one long rope. She moved slowly to the side of the bed, not able to distinguish anything in the darkness. She did not hold any knife, nor was there any concealed in the gown's pocket. Slocum moved till he stood in back of her. She did not hear him; there were very few people who could hear Slocum when he chose to be silent, and all of them were Apache or Comanche trackers. No one else.

She bent over the bed.

"*Don* Alejandro," she whispered.

"*Aquí*," he said.

Any other woman—or man, for that matter—would have been startled. She made no sound.

"Playing games?" she asked coldly, not turning around. That was the kind of remark well-calculated to prove her superiority and his corresponding inferiority. Slocum was

133

not happy being there in a stud capacity. With difficulty he managed to control his rising irritation.

"No." He bent down and kissed the fine fuzz at the nape of her neck. She hadn't expected that, and she gave a little start of surprised pleasure. She wiggled her shoulders, and he kissed her neck once more, this time more firmly. He placed his arm around her till each hard palm was cupping a heavy yet firm breast. The nipples seemed to spring up under his palms like tiny jacks-in-the-boxes.

To his surprise, Slocum felt his penis swell. It was pressed against the white silk that stretched over her buttocks. She began to thrust her hips backwards, grinding them around and around against his penis. She reached down and pulled up her skirt till she was naked from the waist down. Her flesh felt hot and smooth as silk. Her right hand came around and grasping his penis, now rock-hard with excitement, she began to milk it as if it were a cow's udder. Then she flung her head back and her pointed red tongue found his lips, pried them apart, and flicked itself in and out of his mouth.

Slocum had not had a woman since the time when he had first sat down at the same table with Ortega and Arango that night long ago in Brownsville. He had thought that the particular viciousness of this French-woman would eliminate all sexual desire for her. He had grimly started this evening by regarding this night's activity as a performance to go through as if he were an actor in a bad mood, facing a hostile audience. He was startled to discover that he was wrong.

"Get into bed!" she hissed.

"Suppose he misses you?"

She laughed. "Every time he makes love, he goes to sleep. Right away. And he snores till morning. I can't stand him. He makes a few goatlike pushes, yells, and then rolls over. Tonight he made me very hot, because I

134

was thinking of you. I want you to spend a long time. You understand, of course."

Of course I understand, Slocum thought grimly. I had better understand or I will be very sorry.

"Lie on your back!" she commanded. He got into bed. She sank to her knees on the floor and took his penis into her mouth. He had had an erection, but her skillful manipulation of his scrotum with one hand and the simultaneous licking and sliding of her hot, wet mouth up and down the hard shaft of his penis swelled it even more than he thought possible.

She sensed his imminent ejaculation and stopped just in time. She had said "a long time," Slocum remembered, and she meant it. She bent down and licked his scrotum with light, delicate, flicking stabs with her wet tongue. No wonder Gutierrez had told his wife to stay in Paris, in spite of the heavy expenses she must be incurring with the dressmakers.

Ghislaine slid into bed, pulling her gown up to her neck. Her breasts were like two perfect white globes which came to a point, topped with the hard cherries of her erect nipples. She put a pillow under her buttocks and maneuvered him skillfully with her hands until he was kneeling between her lifted thighs. Taking his penis in both her palms, she said, "You will spend a long time making love to me. You will do exactly what I tell you to."

"Yes," Slocum said. He had promised himself that he would do just that.

"Put it in very slowly."

Slocum did as he was told.

"Now all the way, but slowly."

Slocum followed orders.

"Now keep it there."

Likewise.

She had superb muscular control of her vaginal muscles. When she felt he was becoming somewhat limp she began her vaginal contractions. It was like a wet, skillful hand gently squeezing. He became hard once more. She kept him at it for three hours. Slocum knew it was very lucky for him that he had eaten and slept well during the past week; a lackluster performance in that bed would send him to the military barracks where Escalante would settle his hash in his usual nasty way.

Suddenly she was breathing faster and faster. She gripped his back with her long nails and said, "Fuck me! Hard! In and out! Hard! Fast! Faster! Hurt me!"

The last request was a pleasure. Slocum went at it with enthusiasm. He drove his hips against hers as hard as he could, somewhat apprehensive that the slapping of his body against hers might be heard in the corridor outside.

"Harder!" she gasped.

He was afraid she might scream at her climax, but she did not. When she was on the verge of her orgasm, she lifted her legs high, drove her ankles against his lower back, hissed "Come!", raked his back with her nails, and bit his right shoulder as hard as she could, moaning in a long, convulsive shudder. The pain of her nails raking raw gouges across his back infuriated him. If it had been any other woman in the world, he would have slapped her hard. But it was Ghislaine Marchand under him. He grimly set his lips.

The body under him became soft and yielding. "You're too heavy," she said lazily. "Get off."

Orders were orders. He rolled over. She got up, wiped the sweat and semen from herself with his towel, pulled on her gown and padded to the balcony. Slocum got into bed. He was exhausted. The small of his back ached from its unaccustomed activity. He locked his hands behind his neck and stared at her.

At the balcony she turned.

"The contract has been carried out," she said and disappeared. Slocum sighed. His back began to pain him where he had been scratched, but he was so tired that he fell asleep immediately. Another Mexican obstacle removed. Holy Jesus, he thought, what a country!

30

Slocum woke. Someone was tapping very discreetly at his door. Was she back for more? He hoped not. He pulled a sheet around him and walked over.

"*Quien es?*" he said softly.

Back came the whispered response, "*La criada, señor.* The maid."

He unlocked and unbolted the door. It was the same *criada* of last night. Folded over her forearms were fresh bedsheets, a pillow case, and a towel. In her hands she held a basin half full of hot water. Under her armpit she clutched a small box. Slocum closed the door behind her, somewhat puzzled.

She made the bed immediately, replacing the semen-stained sheet. Then she motioned for him to lay face down. She gently swabbed his back and shoulders till they were cleansed of the dried blood. Then she swabbed the deep scratches with iodine, giggling as he cursed under his breath. She next surveyed the room to see if everything was in order. Satisfied, she smiled and withdrew. A pearl, Slocum thought. He hoped that Ghislaine was paying her well. He washed, shaved, and dressed. His back felt much better. He walked downstairs. The gardener had watered the garden, and little drops of water still sparkled on the leaves. The soil smelled fresh, and butterflies were fluttering from flower to flower; the hum of bees filled the air. Slocum decided that if he ever lived long enough to retire, he would like just such a house and such a garden, completely closed off from any passerby's view. He detested the American style of building a house with an elaborate lawn dedicated to impressing the neighbors, and where no one could ever sleep or relax.

Breakfast was served in the *patio* before the sun could begin its murderous ascent. Eggs *rancheros*, café au lait, freshly baked rolls and butter, and fresh papaya and limes. Slocum ate hungrily.

"You eat, *Don* Alejandro," said Ghislaine, "as if the air of Torreón agreed with you very well."

"I find the climate invigorating, *señora*," Slocum responded, keeping his face locked into an amiable expression. She was sitting in a flowered robe—cool, elegant, and remote. Gutierrez sat next to her, proudly holding her hand as he ate.

"Isn't she a beauty?" he demanded. "Do you have anyone like her in the United States?"

"No, we do not, *Don* Aurelio," Slocum said in all sincerity.

"When I look at her," Gutierrez said tenderly, "words fail me."

Words did not fail Slocum, especially on this point. However, he smiled and said nothing. Gutierrez, after all, Slocum knew, would not have much longer to enjoy her. She would move on soon. Torreón was too dull, too confined for her, and when she extracted as much cash or jewels as she could, she would be on her way.

After breakfast she rose. "My dear," said *Don* Aurelio, "we will stay here and talk business. Will you send in Juanito?"

"Of course, *mi amor. Señor*," she said, turning to Slocum, "I wish your venture all success. I understand you are leaving today?"

"Perhaps."

"In that case, *adíos*." She held out her hand. Slocum

138

took her hand for a moment. There was no secret pressure. She had used him for her pleasure, and it was over. Period. A strange, cold woman, he thought. He watched her stroll slowly across the *patio*.

"An extraordinary woman," Slocum said. "I congratulate you, *Don* Aurelio."

Gutierrez flushed with pleasure. "Thank you. Ah, here comes Gomez! Now that we are all here, *Don* Alejandro, I must tell you that Juanito and I discussed the matter last night very carefully. I am very much interested. First, of course, I must take a look at this phosphorus deposit. Everything depends on that."

He was damn right. Everything depends on that, Slocum thought grimly. He felt a quiet jubilation. His whole scheme depended on Gutierrez coming up to Monterrey on this little inspection trip.

"*Naturalmente*," said Slocum courteously.

"We will take the 10:00 A.M. train to Monterrey. I hope this is satisfactory?"

"Of course, *señor*."

"Would you care to pack? We have half an hour before the train leaves."

Slocum rose. He nodded to Gomez and Gutierrez and went up to his room. It would not be necessary to wire Monterrey in order to alert Ortega. Either Ortega or Arango would be at the depot watching every train arrival. Slocum had decided that sending a telegram might be viewed with suspicion by such naturally suspicious people as Gutierrez and Gomez. He packed quickly, feeling relieved that he had said his farewell already to Ghislaine. The woman was unpredictable, and he was somewhat apprehensive as to what she might do.

The coach was waiting inside the *patio*. There were already two men in it, sitting opposite the seat where he and the two financiers would be sitting. Both wore big cone-peaked *sombreros*, tight trousers, and leather leggings. Their big chests had criss-crossed cartridge belts. Each wore two pistols. *Rurales.* Ex-bandits. Very tough. Not good news.

Gutierrez did not bother to introduce them. Noting Slocum's surprised look, Gutierrez said casually, "Many bandits are around. Maybe the train will be held up. One never knows."

"True," said Slocum, pretending admiration for this foresighted behavior.

"I thought it would be a good idea. The colonel lent them to me. We are good friends."

"The colonel?"

"Colonel Escalante. He is in charge of the troops here in Torreón."

Yes, indeed, Slocum thought.

"I would have liked him to meet you, but he is away in the north, looking for this damned rebel, Or-or——" He looked at Gomez for help.

"Ortega," Gomez supplied.

Thank God for Ortega, Slocum thought. If he had had to face Escalante in *Don* Aurelio's house, he didn't think he could get away with the deception.

"Is this Ortega a bandit? Or something more?" asked Slocum.

"A bandit. The worst kind. The man actually had the insolence to issue his own currency! That was how Colonel Escalante almost came to catch him. The angry peons in his area found out that the money was of no value. They went to the *rurales'* commander and led the way to his hideout, but he escaped. We will get him, never fear. His second-in-command was in this very house, you know."

"*Here?*" Slocum demanded, with a startled expression which Gutierrez found gratifying.

"Yes. Colonel Escalante was chatting with him, trying to persuade him to er—cooperate—" Here Gutierrez chuckled. "But the fellow then attempted to strangle my wife, beat her almost to death, and then he escaped."

Slocum shook his head at the vileness of human behavior.

"He was a *gringo* like you."

"Please do not judge us all," Slocum said, "by the behavior of one."

"Of course not, my dear *Don* Alejandro! Ah, here is the depot."

They descended from the coach. As they entered the depot, a middle-aged man with a gray stubble rose from a bench, picked up a battered suitcase, and joined them, with a slight nod toward Gutierrez. He had the indefinable air of a mining engineer; Slocum recognized it right away: a good suit of clothes, hardly ever worn, tanned and seamed face, and strong, calloused hands.

"*Don* Alejandro," said Gutierrez. "Permit me to introduce *Don* Arturo Burton. He is an Englishman. He will come with us to Monterrey."

Burton was a tall, thin man, with a racking cough and two unhealthy-looking red spots in his cheeks. He shook hands silently. Slocum concealed his curiosity. The train pulled in on time. They went aboard and settled down. The two *rurales* sat together on the last seat in the car, so that they could keep an eye on the whole car at once. One of the *rurales* immediately slid his *sombrero* over his eyes and went to sleep, while the other watched, immobile and unblinking, like a huge, dangerous lizard. They could be a problem, Slocum thought. He didn't like them at all, and their presence was something he had not anticipated. Gutierrez was smarter than he had guessed, and this addition of the Englishman was another little surprise he had not counted on. He hoped there would be no slipup once they were all in Monterrey.

The train began to move. Exactly what was, Burton doing aboard? Gutierrez leaned over and answered this

141

question with his next statement. "I hope, *Don* Alejandro, you don't mind if I get an independent opinion on the phosphorus?"

"Of course not," Slocum said calmly. He didn't like the sound of Gutierrez's remark at all.

Gutierrez continued. "*Señor* Burton is a mining engineer."

Just what I feared, goddammit, Slocum thought.

"You two should have plenty to talk about until we get to Monterrey," Gutierrez went on. Like hell they'd find a lot of talk about, Slocum thought grimly. He could persuade a layman that he was a mining engineer, but a *real* mining man could expose him for a fraud with a few minutes' casual conversation and shop talk. Of that Slocum had no doubt whatsoever. So, he knew he would have to avoid conversation with the Englishman at all costs. He closed his eyes and pretended to fall asleep. But something was tapping him on his left knee. He opened his eyes. It was Burton, who had sat down opposite him.

"*Señor* Garrison," he was saying, "where did you get your degree?"

31

Had Gutierrez put Burton up to it? Or was this simply Burton's innocent way of passing the time? Mining men in Mexico rarely came across one another, since the mines were usually so remote and travel was difficult. Maybe the Englishman just wanted to talk shop as the train passed through mile after mile of dull upland scrub *chaparral*. It was hard to say. Burton was sitting opposite, looking at him with interest; Gomez sat next to him so that he could get a good look at Slocum's face and reactions as the two mining engineers chatted, and Gutierrez had swiveled around as he sat beside Slocum. There were, thus, three men staring intently at Slocum. Were they making a deliberate test of his mining-engineer identity, or were they rather bored and wishing to pass the time? Slocum had no idea.

He yawned and stretched, using the gesture as a cover while he looked sharply at the three men. They seemed calm and even a little bored, especially Gomez, who, Slocum was sure, was a naturally suspicious type. Whatever the true situation, the question of his mining degree was one that had to be answered; an evasion would rouse the sleeping dogs of suspicion to immediate alarm.

"Colorado School of Mines," Slocum said, yawning again.

"Good school, that. I went to the University of London and then to Berlin. Did you know Professor Larkin?"

This could be a trick question. That is, there might be *no* Professor Larkin. To say, therefore, that of course he knew the professor would be to expose himself immediately for a fraud. On the other hand, to say he didn't know him, if Professor Larkin existed . . . it was an infuriating dilemma. Slocum sliced the dilemma down the middle.

"Well," said Slocum, "I started at the school, and went a year, taking the basic courses. Then I went broke, so I dropped out for a few years, working in gold mines out in Nevada and California until I had saved up enough money to pay for the rest of my tuition. So maybe Larkin was there when I was out in the field."

Luck was with him. "Yes," Burton said, nodding. "I heard Larkin had gone on to Columbia." He coughed for a long time, burying his face in a dirty handkerchief. He emerged, red-faced and gasping. "I picked up pneumonia in a wet operation," he gasped, "and since then I haven't been able to shake off this damned cold of mine. You worked in mines yourself?"

"Yes. That's when I decided to become an engineer."

143

"How very interesting. I've always been curious about your ore-reduction process. Some day I'll go up to Colorado and see how they do it. But about this phosphorus. In what form did you find it?"

Everything that Slocum knew about phosphorus, he thought ironically, could be written on the head of a match. This was a question that had to be nipped in the bud.

"Mr. Burton," he said drily, "I prefer that you make your own decisions when you see it. Even among engineers, there is frequently ground for disagreement."

"True, true," Burton sighed. "It's good to have company. I've been the only mining engineer in a gold mine in a remote area west of Torreón."

Now that he had found a fellow professional, Slocum was afraid that it would be hard to stop his hunger for talk.

"It is amusing, *Señor* Garrison," Burton said, leaning back and pressing his handkerchief against his lips, "to hear other engineers speak of entering and leaving the Sierra as if it were the same as entering or leaving a dungeon. To me it is home."

Slocum nodded. He did not want Burton to stay on the subject of mining. It would be too easy for an innocent statement or question to become a springboard for a question he wouldn't be able to answer—and with those two *rurales* sitting back of him in the car. . . .

But Burton loved mines. He loved mining. All of Slocum's attempts to deflect him away from that subject failed. Slocum had to be very careful how he did it, with Gutierrez and Gomez listening.

"How did that Sutro Tunnel work out?" Burton demanded. Slocum felt relieved. He had worked one winter on the Comstock Lode, ranging from a little valley below Silver City, all the way up the Lode to Virginia City, and he knew the area well. The Sutro was a five-

144

mile-long tunnel, and it was designed to drain water from the lowest level of the mines which the pumps had become unable to keep in check.

Slocum told him about the Sutro. He told Burton of standing in snow up to his ankles under 100-foot tall pines in the Sierra Nevada and watching the desert along the Carson River quivering in the August heat. He told him of squatting in the icy North Fork of the American River and, with his fingers, scrabbling out gold nuggets from crevices in the rock riverbed—which no one else had thought of trying.

Burton was fascinated. Thank God, Slocum thought, he had stopped asking questions about stopes and mercury reduction. "One must admit," said Burton wistfully, "that stories of gold nuggets are listened to with far more interest than tales of phosphorus mines. But I wanted to ask your ideas on eliminating impurities from various phosphoric compounds. I've heard conflicting stories. There is the catalytic process—" On he went.

Slocum forced himself to listen as if everything that Burton was saying was perfectly self-evident. But he knew that Burton could very well be digging a pit into which he, Slocum, might easily fall and never be able to climb out. The man had to be stopped skillfully.

"*Señor* Burton," he said, lifting a hand. "Let me speak frankly. I have not studied phosphorus since my college days. And they are long past. There will be plenty of time to read all the literature as soon as I get back to my office in San Francisco. In the meantime, since I will be working for the first time in Mexico, there are many questions which only you can answer."

"Yes," said Burton, flattered.

"First of all. The labor supply."

This was Burton's major obsession. He spoke on it an hour, consumed with rage. Slocum then asked him about English pumps versus American pumps. This was good for half an hour. On he went, until finally Slocum yawned, and said, "And now, *señor*, forgive me, I must take my *siesta*."

"Of course."

Slocum closed his eyes. He was not sleeping, but he had passed the test—if it *was* a test—to see if he were really a mining engineer named Garrison. Slocum was sure that the telegrams sent and received by Gomez had taken care of that. So Gutierrez and Gomez were sure. They were snoring. One of the *rurales* was shaking his sleeping partner, whose right hand automatically went to his gun butt as he opened his eyes. Slocum noticed this. They were dangerous men, he knew and there would be a serious problem that night in Monterrey. They looked like Yaquis—big, broad-shouldered men with high cheekbones and quick catlike movements. They would have to be killed before they would stop doing their duty. Mexico was not a country where one played games.

Late that afternoon the train slid into the station at Monterrey. Several coachmen vied for them and their trade, but one coach was bigger and cleaner than all the others. It could easily carry all of them and their luggage.

"*A'onde?*" demanded the *cochero*.

"Posada Carapán," said Slocum. This was a fine, small hotel that he and Ortega had decided upon. It had a fine garden, and a low wall without glass on the top, which could be easily climbed over.

"*Sí, señor.*" The voice was familiar. Slocum leaned forward a bit, as if to look at an old building nearby. It was Ortega. Slocum did not approve of bravado like this. He frowned and sank back in his seat.

"*Cochero!*" Gutierrez said in a commanding, arrogant voice which, Slocum well knew, sent hackles up Ortega's neck. It was too curt, too harsh.

"*Sí, señor.*" Ortega's voice was soft and deferential.

146

Slocum relaxed a bit; he had not known Ortega could act so well. The two *rurales* sat with their backs to Ortega, staring from time to time at the pretty girls. One consolation about Ortega's showing up, Slocum thought: There would be no need to tell him that an added complication had arrived—the two *rurales*. Their rifles lay across their laps, ready for instant action. They looked at the girls, yes, Slocum noticed, but their eyes were watching everything.

"*Cochero*, how well do you know Monterrey?" Oretga, without looking around at Gutierrez, simply held out one arm, and tapped his palm with the forefinger of the other.

Gutierrez laughed. "As well as he knows his own palm," he said, chuckling. Then he demanded, "Do you know the best whorehouse?"

"As God is my witness," Ortega said, "I know the best one in all of Mexico. And it is here, in Monterrey!"

"Good. You will wait for us."

"*Sí, señor.*"

The coach clopped on through the streets. Slocum had never liked Monterrey. Its pace was too fast, too brusque, as if it were trying to imitate Chicago. Its railroad yards were too big. It had none of the graceful, leisurely air of Torreón. But it might become the place where he would recover his lost investment. If this could turn out to be so, he might very well conceive of a sudden affection for the town. The horse clip-clopped on through the cobblestoned streets. To one side rose the mountain called the Bishop's Saddle, and on the other stretched the flat expanse of a town close enough to the United States to be Mexico's main distribution center, a point that had weighed in Gutierrez's decision that it could be a superb area for a mine of almost pure phosphorus. This was one of the big reasons why Slocum had picked Monterrey for Gutierrez. And last, but not least, Slocum thought, it would not be far to the border at all.

Moreover, if the roads to the north and safety would be blocked with federal troops and *rurales* and their unpleasant tendency to shoot first and ask questions later, he could quietly drop south to Tampico and board one of the frequent ships sailing for New Orleans. There were some things highly in favor of Monterrey.

The coach drew up in front of the Posada Carapán. The *rurales* got out first and quickly took a stance with their Mausers at the ready. They watched the street and the passersby with a hard, cold stare, Slocum noticed. A few pedestrians crossed to the other side of the street. *Rurales* meant trouble, and if they were around and started any kind of a fight, they were never reprimanded or punished. It would take some extra planning to deal with them.

"Pay him, Juanito. Give him a good tip. He will wait for us."

"How long, *señor*?" Ortega asked hesitantly.

"Enough to make it worth your while, *hombre*."

Slocum delayed his exit from the coach by pretending to have difficulty getting his cigar to draw.

"We will have to do it at the whorehouse," Ortega said, nodding at the *rurales*. "The hotel is no good with them around." He picked up Slocum's suitcase. "Permit me, *señor*," he said loudly, and jumping down, walked beside Slocum as they entered the Posada.

"Do we have anyone besides Arango?"

"No," said Ortega, surprised. "Three is enough to handle them. Where is your gun?"

"In my suitcase. I'll have it in my belt. I'm a little worried about the *rurales*."

Ortega smiled. "I would not worry," he said, with a hard little smile. "*Rurales* killed Arango's father."

Ortega set down the suitcase and pointed at the big

148

mountain that rose to the east of Monterrey, as if he were a guide showing a tourist the sights. "That, *señor*, is the Bishop's Saddle. Very beautiful view from the top." Gutierrez turned, and seeing that Slocum was apparently interested in being shown the sights, shrugged and walked on."

"They took Arango's father into San Isidro and then untied him. He was very hungry. He had not eaten for three days. The *jefe* of the *rurales* pointed to a Chinese restaurant down the street and asked him if he was hungry. He said yes. The chief gave him a few *pesos* and said, 'Go eat, old man.' The old man was very simple, trusting everyone. He said, '*Gracias, señor.*' There was a *rurale* in each of five doorways across the street. Shot while attempting to escape, no? But all they wanted was to use him for target practice. Arango will take care of the *rurales*, you and I will take care of the other three *cabrónes.*"

" 'Take care of'?"

"Not kill. Just keep them from doing anything foolish."

"You have a place ready?"

"Everything is ready. When you get inside the hotel, tell the two *cabrónes* I'm going to get something to eat and that I'll be right back." Slocum knew that Ortega was going to alert Arango as to the *rurales*. He nodded. Ortega raised his voice for the benefit of any casual bystander. "Moreover, *señor*, nearby are some beautiful waterfalls. Perhaps you would care to see them?"

"Perhaps. I will decide later."

"As you wish."

A maid came and took his suitcase. Slocum followed her to his room. He was changing into a fresh shirt when he heard a knock on his door. "Come in," he called out. Gutierrez entered and asked if he would like to accompany them on the trip to the brothel. "Of course," said Slocum with a smile.

"My wife is very attractive," Gutierrez said, "and I have no complaints, but men do like a change, is it not so?"

Slocum nodded, thinking that Ghislaine would provide so many changes during the course of any one day that any one man would find it difficult to keep up. He would not find it necessary to vary his tastes with any other woman, Slocum thought, if he were involved with the Frenchwoman. He turned to put on a fresh shirt.

"Good God," Gutierrez remarked. "*What* happened to your back?" Slocum cursed himself for forgetting that Ghislaine had scratched him badly. Then he heard Gutierrez chuckling. "Of course," he said, "of course. I heard your door opening during the night; and some time later I heard the maid go down the corridor. I had no idea she was so passionate! There were times— but, perhaps, we had better not discuss this!"

Slocum decided to do nothing except to smile knowingly while he put on his shirt.

"You will be down soon?" asked the Mexican.

Slocum nodded, and Gutierrez withdrew.

As soon as he had left the room, Slocum ferreted out his Colt from his suitcase and stuck it in his belt. He then surveyed the contents of the suitcase. He would not see this room again, nor would he see the suitcase. It had served its purpose well. No, there was nothing in it he wanted. He left the room and walked down the wide staircase. At the landing he stopped to observe some blue tiles which had been set into the gray stone floor in a compass design. He stared at the north-pointing arrow. With any luck he would be heading in that direction in a few days.

He continued down the stairs to the *patio*. The others were seated there, drinking *tequila*. The two *rurales* lounged against the gate, one staring at the street, the other continually scanning the walls and the roof. Good

150

men, Slocum thought again. He sat down under a palm, the back of his chair pushing against a mass of flowering pink oleander. Lavishly blooming bougainvillea grew up the rough stucco surface of the wall. He ordered lemonade; he could not afford to have his judgment clouded by alcohol.

"We've been waiting," Gutierrez said with annoyance.

"I'm sorry, *señors*. I was extremely dusty."

"It's just a whorehouse, *Don* Alejandro, not a formal dinner at the Presidential Palace!"

Slocum silently thanked God that the phosphorus deal was not a real one. He did not think he could have stood Gutierrez's mood changes, which were becoming more and more irritating. The man had been pleasant only three minutes before when he had come up to Slocum's room; now, under some sort of pressure to visit the brothel, he was busily finding fault. It would be a pleasure to see the way Gutierrez would handle himself later in the day, after Arango had taken care of the *rurales*.

Gomez permitted himself a sour, discreet smile. It was clear to Slocum that the man was taking a malicious pleasure in hearing someone else get a bawling-out.

Gutierrez did not have sense enough to let it drop. Like a nagging woman, he could not stop, even though he had made his point. "Monterrey is not Mexico City, *Don* Alejandro," he went on. "You seem to think it obligatory to pretend you are going to be the guest of honor at a big party!"

I'm not—*you* are, thought Slocum. Burton was embarrassed at being forced to hear this outburst. Turning pink, he stared at his glass. Slocum found the outburst very interesting. It meant that Gutierrez, sure that he would be apprised tomorrow of the location of the mine, now felt that he could dispense with Slocum. He had his own mining engineer with him, who could verify the accuracy of Slocum's description; he was convinced that his friendship with Díaz would ensure that the option would drop into his outstretched hand like a ripe apple. If these things were so, and it certainly looked as if they were, why in God's name and all the saints was it necessary to curry favor with the stupid *gringo* engineer from San Francisco?

"I really am sorry, *señors*," Slocum said, placatingly. He sipped his lemonade.

Gutierrez was mollified. "All right," he said briefly, and then added, with some residual rancor, "just don't let it happen again."

Slocum's amusement was now replaced with growing anger. The arrogant son of a bitch! he thought. Imagine what the man would have been like if there really *had* been a mine; if *he* had really been a mining engineer with a sincere, honest proposal. Not only would he be thoroughly screwed à la mexicana, but he'd also be continually spoken to as if he were a stupid waiter in a fourth-rate restaurant in which the great Mexican financier happened to be unfortunately condemned for a meal. Gutierrez deserved a harsh lesson for what he might have done had Slocum been an honest American engineer—and Slocum was very happy that he, Slocum, would personally be conducting a class in etiquette that very evening.

32

It was late in the afternoon, and too early for the evening's trade. The girls were getting up, yawning, bathing, eating breakfast, or sewing and ironing. When the coach drove into the courtyard, many of them were engaged in combing their long, lustrous black hair.

But they were delighted that so many customers had

arrived, customers who looked rich. They filed into the ornate, plush parlor and sat down on the overstuffed Victorian furniture. They tried to look demure, for this was, after all, by common consent, the best whorehouse in the entire state of Tamaulipas. Slocum tried to persuade the two rurales to take girls and go off to their rooms, telling them he would be happy to pay for the pleasure of such efficient guards, but Gutierrez curtly refused permission.

"No, *gracias*, *Don* Alejandro," one said regretfully. "Many thanks, but we are on duty. Many thanks, *señor*." They sat stiffly in the parlor, their Mausers across their knees, looking yearningly at the half-naked women.

"Are we to be robbed?" Slocum demanded with a smile.

"One never knows, *señor*," the man said seriously.

One never knew, indeed. Slocum wished they were on his side. He picked a girl and went to her room. She reeked of cheap perfume. She pulled off her dress and lay back on her embroidered coverlet, her fingers idly toying with the stitching. Slocum removed a cheap enameled wash basin from a crudely made chair and sat down. She had big breasts with enormous dark-brown aureolas and the small, delicate, narrow feet of Mexican women. She stared at him in surprise.

"You're not coming to bed, *señor*?"

"No, *señorita*."

"Well, then!" She started to get up. If he didn't screw her, she wouldn't get any money. She resented undressing for nothing, and she made this clear.

The usual fee was two *pesos*. The house took half. Slocum gave her ten. She stared at him again, puzzled and suspicious.

"I am *very* tired, *señorita*. I shall wait till my friends leave. Shall we talk?"

153

"If you wish." She didn't like customers who wanted to talk instead of screwing. She *liked* to screw. This customer was very handsome, and when he picked her she was flattered and excited at the thought of his making love to her. She clasped her hands behind her neck and stared at the ceiling. Her breasts were firm. Slocum thought he might have changed his mind about sleeping with whores, except that he did not want to be naked when the time came for fast action.

"*Momentito*," said Slocum. "Where is the toilet?"

"In the back, downstairs," she said, wondering what kind of a weird customer she had this time.

Slocum got up and walked downstairs to the parlor. Ortega was sitting there, chatting idly with the *rurales*. When he saw Slocum, he stood up. "*Buenas tardes, señor*," he said. "The girls are pretty, no?"

"Yes, *hombre*. You certainly told the truth."

Behind Ortega's back, Slocum saw Arango come shuffling in. He stopped at the door and braced himself with both arms against the doorjamb. He was pretending to be drunk, Slocum saw immediately. He was dressed like a *peon*, with a machete in a leather scabbard slung across his shoulders. From one hand there hung an old, battered, cheap guitar.

"Oh, oh," said Ortega. "*Uno borrachito!* A little drunken man! Watch the madam throw him out, *señor*. *Señora!*" he called out loudly. "*Señora! Un cliente!*"

Arango gave a very good imitation of a magnificently drunk peon. He slid halfway down the jamb, managed to pull himself erect with much grunting, took a few steps, stumbled across a table, fell, stood up, tripped over a chair, stood up, and lurched across the room, his guitar banging and thrumming as he moved. The *rurales* were vastly amused. But Slocum noticed that each of Arango's apparently haphazard movements was bringing him closer and closer to the two unsuspecting *rurales*.

154

"My friend," said Ortega with a grin, "you will break your beautiful and valuable guitar. Permit me." He stood up and took the guitar from Arango, who stared at him with his mouth half-open in his dazed, drunken face.

The madam entered the room. She was a buxom woman of 60 with elaborately arranged black-dyed hair and a pair of brilliant black eyes, which were now narrowed in anger.

"*Borracho!*" she hissed in fury. "Get out!"

The *rurales'* attention was now diverted to her. They stared at her, grinning and enjoying her anger. This was the moment for which Arango and Ortega had been waiting. From the rear, Ortega lifted the guitar and smashed it over the head of the *rurale* nearest to him, and simultaneously Arango straightened up, lifted up his coarse white peon blouse, jerked a Colt, and fired four shots very fast, two in each *rurale*'s chest.

The two men slid sidewards in their chairs, still alive. Before they reached the floor, Arango had jumped beside them, wrenched their Mausers away, and then gave each man a vicious and unnecessary kick, paying no attention to the madam's screams. They toppled to the floor, staring up in hatred at Arango, who returned their look with interest.

"As soon as you enter hell, motherfuckers," he hissed in a cold, icy voice, with a level of cold hatred that Slocum had never heard in his life, "take the first left turn. You will find a Chinese restaurant." They died uncomprehending.

Ortega had already began to take the stairs two at a time as soon as he had brought down Arango's guitar. Slocum was right behind him. Ortega burst into Gomez's room, while Slocum entered Gutierrez's. The man was busily pulling on his pants.

"What is it, a robbery?" Gutierrez gasped. An oily sweat had oozed all over his hairy, fat body.

"No," Slocum said soothingly. "Get dressed. It is not a robbery."

"What happened? Where's the *rurales*?"

"The *rurales*? Dead."

"*Dead?*"

"Yes, dead," he said sharply. "Do not make me repeat it. Or I will have to consider you a thick-headed son of a bitch. Gutierrez, I would prefer to consider you a gracious and intelligent host."

Gutierrez was not stupid. He now knew that Slocum must have been involved in whatever had happened, since one of the *rurales'* Mausers was now pointing at his stomach.

"Pay the girl," Slocum said.

"I already did."

"Pay her again," Slocum said, grinning.

Gutierrez paid her again. She stopped trembling long enough to smile.

"How is he in bed?" Slocum asked.

"*Ay! Uno cabrito!*" she exclaimed. "A little goat!"

Slocum smiled and pushed Gutierrez at the end of the Mauser into the parlor. Gomez and Burton stood there, pale and nervous as they stared at the two dead *rurales*. "All here!" Slocum observed cheerfully. He extracted Gutierrez's wallet from his pocket. Ortega and Arango had tied their prisoners' hands behind their backs with short lengths of rawhide. The madam stood rigid and disapproving while Arango pulled out another piece of rawhide from his pants and tied Gutierrez's hands behind his back and shoved him out of the house toward the coach in the *patio*. Slocum lingered behind.

"*Señora*," he said, removing the cash from Gutierrez's wallet, "you will be asked many questions after we leave." He handed her 2000 *pesos*, and he gave each of the girls 200. "We would be grateful if you say that

156

ten men came on horseback. We were all Indians. You think Yaquis. But you are not sure. We rode to the west. If you say this, we will come back and give you the same amount that you are now receiving. If you tell the truth, we will come back some day for a visit." Slocum was a great believer in winning friends via the economic route. He bowed, *"Buenas tardes, señora y señoritas!* Call the police in an hour, please."

"Buenas tardes, señor," they murmured. The conflicting stories that the police—and the *rurales*—would get from the women would be enough to confuse the pursuers for a day or so; enough for a good start.

The three prisoners lay flat on their backs in the middle of the coach, gagged and blindfolded. Ortega had thrown an old horse blanket over them, and a casual look into the coach would reveal nothing. Arango was already far ahead, trotting along on his stolen horse. Ortega cracked his whip and the coach pulled away. He leaned back in his seat and rested his feet on Gutierrez's plump belly.

"And what else is there to see in Monterrey, *cochero?"* Slocum demanded.

"If your honor wishes," Ortega said, "I can recommend a remote waterfall."

"Vamonos!"

33

The ransom had been agreed upon: 200,000 dollars in United States ten-dollar bills.

There was no reason to hold Gomez, who, moreover, could vouch for the fact that it was a bona fide kidnapping. Also, his word would be acceptable to the bank. And Burton? Why hold him? Slocum saw no reason.

After all, the poor man had been dragged down from his mine and all the way up to Monterrey on a wild-goose chase.

Ortega had located an abandoned woodcutter's hut two miles up a forest trail from the waterfall. He had stocked it with food. There was no corn grown in the area, and hence there were no farms—and no villages. The result was that no one would see them come and go.

That same night, Gomez and Burton were blindfolded once more. They were led down the trail on foot and placed in the coach, which Ortega had hidden under the trees. Slocum tied a horse to the rear of the coach for his return trip.

"*Señor* Burton," Slocum said, handing the Englishman 1000 *pesos* of Gutierrez's money," I'm sorry you were brought out here on a wild-goose chase. I hope this will take care of your expenses. If the fat *cabrón* is released, he will forget all about them, or be too busy to listen to you. So I am taking care of them right now. I wouldn't mention this to him if you ever see him later. He would ask for the thousand back."

"That he would."

"You will not mind walking eight kilometers back to Monterrey? We will let you off somewhere near the town."

"Well—not really. But tell me, is there *actually* a phosphorous mine?"

"No. And I am not a mining engineer."

"You had me fooled. You certainly did."

"If we ever meet—in the States that is—let us say hello. But not in Mexico, if you please. Disease can strike very quickly down here."

"Yes, of course. I have enjoyed our professional association, Mr.—er——"

"Garrison will do."

Slocum turned and gave Gomez 200 *pesos*. "Your

158

expenses," he said. "When you're back in Torreón, think of the fat tub of lard eating very little and sleeping on the stony ground on a thin blanket."

A tiny smile leaked onto Gomez's lips, but he said nothing.

"And give my regards to *Señora* Gutierrēz. I've enjoyed her hospitality and kindness more than I can say."

"I will, *señor*."

"Then *adiós*. I hope to see you soon. You understand the instructions?"

"Yes," Gomez said calmly. "Use bills not in sequence. Put them in a suitcase. Tie suitcase with rope so it won't open accidentally. Take 6:00 P.M. train from Saltillo for Monterrey. Stand on rear platform. When I see two lanterns on the right side of the track, drop suitcase." ·

"And?"

"No attempt to follow. If that happens, you will kill *Señor* Gutierrez."

"Exactly. A week should bring you back. Each day more than a week will see a part of *Don* Aurelio mailed back to you."

Slocum did not mean this. He had never done such a thing, nor would he permit it, although he knew that Arango would have been delighted with the idea of removing Gutierrez's fingers, one by one. But Gomez did not know that Slocum was not the dismembering type.

"That is the road to Monterrey," Slocum said, pointing. "Two hours' walk should bring you there. Good luck." He and Ortega watched the two men trudge downhill. When they had rounded a curve and were out of sight, Ortega took the coach to Monterrey by another road, returned the coach to the livery stable owner from whom he had rented it as a free-lance coachman, and paid the rental fee. Then he walked to the market, bought two lanterns, some kerosene, shoved them in a *sisal morral* he had slung over his right shoulder, and with a machete in its leather scabbard on his left shoulder, plodded out of Monterrey, looking exactly like a peon who had come into town and who was now hiking to his hut in the mountains.

Gutierrez was kept constantly tied up. It was not necessary to blindfold him. They would not return to the hut, and he knew what they looked like anyway.

On the second day from his lookout position atop a tree high up in the mountain, Arango saw the patrols. It was in preparation for just this possibility that Ortega had laid in a supply of jerky and cooked *tortillas*. Nothing required any cooking, for smoke would mean people were there; as it was, they passed by, completely unaware of the trail leading up the mountain from the waterfall.

On the fourth day, Arango, whose nerves were stretching more and more with the tension, burst out with a remark.

"Why the hell wait a week? Look at all the time it gives them to look for us! And why come here? There's too many roads and they're too close. And we're too close to the railroad. They could bring lots of soldiers here very fast. I don't like it. Shit, shit, shit!"

Slocum did not like playing nursemaid to nervous people. He concealed his irritation but with some difficulty. He had been cleaning and oiling his Colt, as he did every few days. He had seen too many guns misfire in critical situations.

"Listen, Luis. To get that money in American dollars——"

"Who wants American dollars? Why not get gold *pesos*! That's real money!"

"Didn't you hear Ortega and me talk about this?"

"I was sleepy," Arango growled.

"All right! Fifty-*peso* gold coins—do you know how

much that will weigh? No? *Twenty thousand!* Want to carry them? No? So we want good American paper money. The Torreón bank doesn't have that kind of money. So it will have to send to El Paso for it. Now, with American money, in a big city, no questions will be asked. If you want to change it to Mexican money, banks are glad to take it. And the money in paper will fill one small suitcase. We can move fast with only one suitcase. Have you ever tried riding fast with a few hundred pounds of gold? I have. It's paper for me. Now, it takes one day for Gomez to talk to the bank and persuade them that Gutierrez has really been kidnapped. A day to go to El Paso, another day for the American bankers to get the money together, and another day to bring it to Monterrey."

"That's only *four* days!"

"*Claro*. We give them three *more* days, because something is always going wrong in this goddamn country."

Slocum was annoyed at having to repeat himself. Arango jerked his head up at the insult to Mexico, as if the remark had lit a fuse inside his head. But at that moment a cry from Ortega, high in the tree overhead on sentry duty, stopped him.

"*Oye!* Alexander the Great! Your turn!"

Ortega had been vastly amused at Slocum's choice of the name "Alexander," and he now used it all the time. Arango's fuse sputtered out. Ortega dropped from the last branch, completely unaware how close his two confederates had come to a serious brawl. Neither Slocum nor Arango mentioned it to him. Slocum walked over to the tree, placed his hands on the branch, and prepared to climb up to his sentry post. Five more days, he thought. I hope we survive. He began climbing.

They survived. It was the fifth night. The moon had not yet risen. They had taken their horses, their supplies, and their weapons. Gutierrez, his hands tied in front of him, was forced to walk the 12 miles to the railroad at the end of a *reata*. He complained bitterly, but Arango silenced him brutally and effectively with a single vicious slash of a braided quirt across Gutierrez's face.

The train was due at the rendezvous point chosen for the lantern signal at a little after 9:00 P.M. No one had a watch, but Slocum, like all people who lived continuously in the open, could always judge the time within a 15-minute range. They were at the railroad by 8:30. Slocum lit the lanterns and immediately covered them with a thick mat made of branches.

"What's the good of that?" demanded Arango. "How are they going to see them from the train?"

Ortega sighed. He explained that if there were patrols watching the tracks they could easily spot the lanterns and thus spoil the operation. "And if they come at us, *Don* Aurelio," he said genially, turning to Gutierrez, who was sitting uncomfortably on a pile of stones, "we will cut your throat so fast you will not know what has happened." Gutierrez's face whitened.

"They will not do it," he said nervously.

"Let us hope so," Ortega said kindly.

Arango would not drop the subject of the lanterns. "I still don't think it's a good idea," he said stubbornly.

Slocum let out a short, exasperated laugh, but said nothing. Arango tensed angrily, but Ortega said, "*Ay, Díos!* Luis, shut up! We'll all be rich soon. *Don* Alejandro will buy guns for us again. We'll have a big army. So *shut up!*"

Slocum's share was 75,000 dollars. The guns would *not* be bought with his money. He had made that absolutely clear. He would act, he said, as Ortega's agent; he would use Ortega's share and make a normal gunrunner's profit, but he was through investing any more of his own money in Mexico.

Far away they heard the train whistle. As soon as the engine passed, they pulled the branches away from the two lanterns. A suitcase sailed from the last car and fell between the rails with a heavy thud.

"Blow out the lanterns!" Slocum ordered. Arango blew them out. In complete darkness, Ortega felt for the suitcase and picked it up, grunting. "It's heavy," he muttered. "I hope it's not a bunch of old Bibles."

"Let's get out fast," Arango said. "I don't like it here."

They mounted and rode in silence to the south across the scrub pine and *chaparral* flats, while Gutierrez trotted behind, panting and moaning with the exertion. In 20 minutes they found a narrow *arroyo* where it would be safe to light the lanterns. Arango let the *reata* slip from the pommel.

"Sit down, pig," he said. Gutierrez collapsed to the ground. Slocum lit a lantern and watched Arango pull out his vicious knife and slice open the suitcase.

"No wonder it was so heavy," Ortega said, but he said it with a smile. There were quite a few 50-*peso* gold coins. A note on the top said:

Señors: I could not get all the necessary paper money. Therefore, 25,000 dollars is in gold. I hope you will find this satisfactory. Gomez.

"*Mierda!*" said Ortega. He turned to Gutierrez. "*Don Aurelio,*" he said politely, "do you have any objection to this gold? We await your response with fear and some trembling."

"No," Gutierrez said shortly, looking at the contents of the suitcase with a pained expression.

"Let's count," Slocum said. He had unsaddled his horse; now he spread the saddle blanket on the ground. In the light of the lantern, he dumped out the suitcase, and swiftly counted. There was no mistake.

"Good man, Gomez," Slocum said, grinning. Gutierrez's face hardened. Someone would catch hell, and the nearest one would be Gomez. Slocum was glad that he had given the man two hundred *pesos*. The secret knowledge of that donation would be some compensation when Gutierrez would begin nagging and fault-finding on his return. Slocum cut Gutierrez's bonds. The fat man began rubbing his wrists. Arango began coiling his *reata* regretfully. He had enjoyed watching *Don* Aurelio groan and pant behind him.

"*Adiós, señor,*" Slocum said. He had been amply repaid for that first painful night he had spent under Gutierrez's roof. Arango now turned Gutierrez so that he faced Monterrey.

"In the *dark*?" he said, obviously terrified.

"Why not?" said Slocum. "There'll only be wolves, mountain lions, and rattlesnakes." "*Vaya con Dios.*"

Arango said, "*Adiós, maricón,*" and kicked him as hard as he could.

Gutierrez fell on his knees, cut them on a sharp stone, and got up painfully. Slocum observed this with disgust. He did not strike unarmed prisoners. They watched Gutierrez hobble awkwardly toward the glow in the northeastern sky which was the night aspect of Monterrey at a distance. He would reach there about sunrise. They rode south for a little while, knowing that this was the direction which Gutierrez would report to the first patrol commander he would see in the morning. Then, after half an hour, they swung to the north, and, led by Ortega, arrived about midnight in a small, grassy valley. While the horses grazed in the moonlight, which was almost strong enough to read by, Slocum spread his saddle blanket once more and made the division.

Allowing for the exchange rate of gold *pesos* against American dollars, the amount was honestly counted. Ortega asked if Slocum objected to taking gold *pesos* in part payment. Slocum did not. He took 4000 dollars in 20-*peso* gold coins and 71,000 dollars in ten-dollar bills. It made a heavy pile. He stuffed the paper money in the saddlebags that Ortega had given him, poured the gold coins into the *sisal morral* which Ortega had brought back from the market in Monterrey, and hung it over his saddlehorn.

"The horse and saddle are yours, *Don* Alejandro," Ortega said, when Slocum offered to pay for them. "I am sorry that things did not work out well after our glorious beginning up in Juárez. Well, we will try again. I am talking to people. Some have already joined me; they are sleeping over there in their *serapes*. Most have no weapons, but we rely upon you to change that. When I am ready to start again, I will send someone to see you—but where will you be?"

"General Delivery, El Paso. I'll pick it up sooner or later."

"Well, then, *adiós!*" Ortega gave Slocum the *abrazo*, hugging him and clapping him on the back at the same time. Slocum returned the *abrazo*—after all, he did like Ortega. Arango did not offer the *abrazo*. Thank God, Slocum thought, the man, at least, was honest in his likes and dislikes. Slocum nodded to Arango. With difficulty, Arango nodded stiffly in return. Then he turned his horse's head to the north.

Three nights' hard riding, holing up by day, would bring him to the Rio Grande. He was in a long, narrow valley, where the trail led through dense stands of ocotillo and smoke-bush from time to time. The moon was all the way up now, and the wind was blowing that blend of damp soil and sagebrush that Slocum always found as exhilarating as a woman's perfume. The horse moved surely along the trail. It was a fine chestnut, no doubt stolen a few days before he and Gutierrez arrived for the phosphorus mine.

The phosphorus mine! Slocum grinned. He had come

out of it all right, but there were simply too many problems to contend with for a *gringo* dealing in Mexico. The profit of a big gun deal was tempting, but it would be too closely run for comfort. It would be wiser to buy cattle legitimately and resell them the same way. His profit would be less, but his nights would be peaceful. And safe. Let someone else raise the cattle, worm them, brand them, stay up nights to catch rustlers, worry all through droughts and those blue northers—all he would do was buy them from ranchers and resell them to stockyards or other ranchers who needed seed stock. His office would be his hat. He was enjoying his daydreaming . . . still, that Marchand woman! If he were to run down to Mexico City in two or three months after his next operation, and take a vacation down there—and wearing a mustache, maybe dyeing his hair—and if she happened to be there—oh, Slocum thought, it was certainly tempting to think about. The way she had ground her hips against his. . . .

Two men burst from the dense growth of ocotillo beside the trail, their machetes swinging high up in the moonlit air. Slocum saw their blades glinting as he spurred the chestnut and grabbed his Colt. One of the machetes sliced through the *morral* at his saddlehorn in its vicious downward sweep. Handfuls of the gold coins cascaded onto the trail. He had pointed the Colt at the man and pulled the trigger. But only a click sounded. For a second, Slocum thought it was a misfire, but when it happened again he knew it was not. He knew what the trouble stemmed from: Arango had removed the bullets while Slocum and Ortega were busily counting the money. And why should he do that? Because Ortega and Arango knew that Slocum would meet the three *macheteros* in a few minutes. All this flashed through Slocum's brain in less than a second.

Another man jumped into the trail, yelling and waving

his machete. The chestnut swerved, then pivoted. The third man ran toward the horse's rear, while the other two were coming for Slocum and lifting their machetes once more. Slocum spurred the chestnut, hoping to ride them down, but as they fell under the horse, the two men slashed hard. One stroke cut Slocum across the top of his left thigh, and the other buried itself in the chestnut's neck. The horse ran at full speed, the blood spurting from a severed artery, covering Slocum with its musty spray. He let the horse run; he had nothing to fight back with. A quarter of a mile was as far as the horse got before it floundered to a halt, trembled, and collapsed suddenly on its right side. It shuddered once and then died. Slocum was pinned underneath by his wounded leg. He worked with frantic haste to extricate himself before the men would come looking for him, in order to machete him to death at their leisure.

34

He finally managed to pull his leg out. He crawled on his hands and knees into the bush, and then he hobbled as far and as fast as he could, listening intently for sounds of pursuit. There were none. He had to do something quickly to stop the bleeding. He halted, sat down, tore his shirt into strips, and bound the slash in his thigh as tightly as possible, making a pressure bandage. He silently thanked God that the blood was flowing evenly, not leaping up in spurts.

Then he moved closer to the trail. No sound. Closer. He crouched so that he could see any moving outline against the sky, and in order to deny anyone looking for him the same vantage. Still there was no one. Slocum sat and considered. Of course, the horse had run away at full speed. They had no way of knowing that it was a fatal wound. They could not possibly follow a good horse since they were on foot, and besides, think of all those lovely gold *pesos* scattered on the trail! After they had done that little chore, each of the three *macheteros* would bury his particular share. Then they would go back and tell Ortega that the goddamn son of a whore *gringo* had gotten away. One or more of them had been hurt when the chestnut had ridden them down; they could show the bruises to Ortega as proof that the *gringo* had escaped. Slocum managed to work loose the saddlebags with his 71,000 dollars. He thought ironically he was a man with a small fortune and there wasn't a doctor around he could call upon for some stitches. He worked his way back from the trail, and several hundred feet away he found a loose, rocky outcrop. He pried loose a few rocks, placed the saddlebags in such a way that they would be protected from rain, and covered them up again. Even if someone would be passing by—which was most unlikely—there would be no signs that any of the rocks had been disturbed. He clambered painfully back to the trail, found a tree, and broke off a dead branch. Placing the fork of it under his arm, he began to hobble painfully back to Ortega's camp. He had some unfinished business.

It took him four hours. He limped in a little after sunrise. There was a sentry sitting atop a huge rock, cradling the *rurales'* Mausers. He stared open-mouthed at Slocum as he shouted "*Quien es?*" Slocum had forgotten that he was covered with the chestnut's blood.

"I want to see General Ortega," he said thickly.

"*Que pasa, hombre?*"

"Ortega! Yes or no?"

"*Momentito.*" He slid off the rock and came back in 15 seconds. "*Por aqui, señor.*"

Ortega was sitting up in his blanket, rubbing his eyes and yawning.

"In the name of God, *Don* Alejandro, what happened?"

The man was a superb actor, Slocum thought. Arango was squatting nearby, pissing. He stood up, buttoned his fly, stared bright-eyed at the blood, and continued boiling coffee in an old tin can. He said nothing, but limited his visible reaction to a faint grin. He did not look surprised. So, then, it was very likely Arango knew about the attack. He didn't participate. Ortega probably planned the whole thing, but, just in case it wouldn't work out, sent out three men with machetes; this would insure, in case of a failure, that Slocum would think it a spontaneous robbery by three local peons.

"Three men attacked me," Slocum said, watching the two narrowly. This had been treason, and Slocum reserved his most violent hatred for that.

"I must admit that I was somewhat worried when you rode off alone," Ortega said solicitously. "My God, have you bled so much? Somebody bring water!"

Someone fetched a bucket of water. Slocum stripped and rinsed the blood out of his clothes. Arango watched him with the smile that never ceased to infuriate Slocum: It was a hard, mocking expression. Arango took the tin can from the fire, and breaking off a lump of brown sugar from a chunk that was lying, covered with flies, on the ground at his feet, dropped it in the coffee. He said, with a grin, "So they got you in the leg?"

Slocum was boiling inside with rage. He made no answer.

"A pity, *Don* Alejandro," Arango said.

I know what you mean by that, you son of a bitch bastard! Slocum thought. But it was necessary to dissemble for the present. Later on, and he would pick the time carefully, he would express himself frankly. Very frankly.

"Yes. I am afraid it was some of your men."

"*Mine*? That is not likely," Ortega said, stiffening. "My men are peons who can no longer tolerate the oppression under which they exist! They——"

Slocum held up his hand. His leg was throbbing and it hurt like hell. "*Mi general*," he said, keeping his voice calm, "that remark will look well on a ten-*peso* note. But consider: This is a road where hardly anyone travels. And certainly not at night. How is it that three men were waiting in the trail just when I rode by? It cannot be coincidence."

"You may be right," Ortega said slowly. "I am distressed at the thought that some of my men may have gotten drunk and attacked you. Did they take all your money?"

"Yes. They cut the saddlebags and the *morral* loose, and my horse ran. The horse died later, but, you see, they thought the horse was still alive."

"Ah," Ortega said, his face darkening. It was clear to Slocum that the men had not mentioned taking the gold; it would be interesting to lay the blame for taking everything on the three *macheteros* and see how they would try to wiggle out of it. Arango's face had swelled with suppressed rage. The three men, he was thinking, had taken all the money, hidden it, and since Slocum had disappeared with his horse and would try to get away from that part of Mexico as quickly as possible. . . . It was easy for Slocum to see Arango's mind working. It was exactly the kind of thing Arango would have done himself had he been in their place.

"Now," Slocum continued, "one of those sons of whores probably was sitting near us last night when we were counting the money for the second time. One of the bastards you said were nearby in their *serapes* reached out and took out the cartridges when I had the belt off." Ortega nodded.

Arango said nothing, but a curious hard glitter came into his eyes.

"You must admit," Ortega said, "that it was a most sensible act."

"True. Even animals can perform tricks." Slocum said this in a deliberate attempt to anger Arango. There was no doubt in his mind that he had succeeded. The man's stomach drew back three inches from his belt buckle, as if to make room for a snake's head that was coiled there and had risen to strike. After a few seconds, the tension lessened. It was not the time yet to deal with Slocum, Arango was thinking.

"I think it would be a good idea to search everyone," Arango said. "No?"

"Good!" Ortega said, slapping his thigh. He ordered everyone to strip. There were 14 men. They stood in a rough semblance of a line and handed their clothes over to Arango, who carefully went through their pockets. The men slouched and grinned at Slocum.

Slocum limped closer. Three of the men had massive bruises. Slocum examined them more closely. Two of the men had horseshoe-shaped bruises. These would be the two men whom his chestnut had ridden down. The third man had a bruise covering his entire upper body at the level where the moving of a horse at full speed, could have struck it.

"How did you get those bruises?" Slocum politely asked the three men.

They grinned and shrugged. The third man was somewhat smarter. He said, "We were thrown out of a *pulquería* in Monterrey. We were very drunk. They beat us. Oh, *señor*, we were *very* drunk." As he spoke, Slocum noticed that he looked at Ortega, as if he wanted his words to win approval.

"The name of the *pulquería?*"

"What, *señor*?"

"Tell me the name of the *pulquería*, please."

"It's—it's—" the man frowned.

"Was it *'Life Is Bitter'*?"

"*Sí, sí!* That was it, *señor*," the man said, with relief.

Slocum turned and limped to Ortega. "I've had enough of this comedy," he said. "These men were ridden down by my horse, and there is no such *pulquería* in Monterrey."

"Are you satisfied that these are the men?"

"Without doubt. I would like them questioned until they reveal the hiding place of my money."

"*Naturalmente, señor.*"

Ortega's face was red with suppressed anger. There was no doubt in Slocum's mind that the general would personally take a deep interest in any questioning—and that the questions would be blunt. Moreover, the accused had absolutely no goddamn legal rights whatsoever, Slocum knew. He felt no pity for the three men who stood there grinning, safe in their complicity.

Ortega turned to Arango. "These men have attacked our good friend, Luis," he said quietly and almost with sadness. "They have dishonored us. And moreover, they have taken his money. Please try and persuade them to return it."

"*Vamonos, chicos,*" Arango said, almost genially, as if he were proposing a game of catch with the three men. The three men turned and, followed by Arango, walked off naked into the morning. Slocum turned and looked questioningly at Ortega.

"They're going for a little *paseo*," Ortega said. "A little walk down the trail, a little conversation to refresh their memories, and everything will be straightened out. In the meantime, you must be fed, *Don* Alejandro," he added, beaming with renewed joviality. "*Comida, pronto!*" he shouted. "Someone bring us food!"

172

In a few minutes Slocum was hungrily munching *tortillas* and broiled beefsteak and sipping coffee, black and sweet and strong, listening to Ortega's cheerful shop-talk about the difficulties of running a successful revolution: the misunderstandings everywhere prevalent, the betrayals that were a constant factor, the impossibility of trusting anyone too long.

"Take Arango," he said. "The crazy fool likes to empty his Colt and he spends all his time snapping the trigger. He likes the sound it makes. He is like a little boy, but he is a very dangerous little boy. I trust him, but he does foolish things from time to time, and then I have to go around apologizing and paying money to keep people quiet. But who is better than Arango to take trains and run them? Ah, what a sad world it is, *Don* Alejandro, that we cannot shape our helpers exactly the way we want them! There comes Luis now. I hope he has good news."

Slocum turned and put down his tin coffee mug. Arango was sauntering toward them with his usual arrogant grin. He nodded at them and jerked his head behind him. Ortega rose, and said, "Would you like to take a brief walk with us, *Don* Alejandro?"

They walked down the trail. A few hundred yards from the camp they stopped in a small clearing. Each of the three naked men had been tied to a small tree trunk, and in front of each one was a small pile of gold coins. "I think you will find that is the correct amount, *señor*," Ortega said. Slocum counted. It was all there. "They volunteered to tell Luis where they had hidden it," Ortega went on. "Very close to the camp." He shook his head, as if aghast at such evil carryings-on.

"Volunteered?" Slocum asked dryly.

Ortega shrugged. "With a little help." The men were pale and even more badly bruised than before. "But," he said, "Luis tells me that they refused to say anything about the American paper money. He thinks they think if he was told about the small amount of gold that we would forget about the paper money." He smiled. "Oh, such children!" he said, shaking his head in amazement. He had taken another *morral* with him; now he handed it to Slocum, who filled it with the gold coins. "I appreciate this," Slocum said.

Ortega shrugged. "Let us go back to camp," he said. "Luis would like to ask them a few more questions about the paper money."

They walked back. At a bend in the path, Slocum turned around, just in time to see Arango pull his knife out of its sheath. He turned around again. He was sorry for the three men, but not too sorry. They had, after all, tried to kill him. And if Ortega knew that he, Slocum, still had the paper money, Arango might be very well preparing to torture him to find out its hiding place. Better to let Ortega think that the money had being hidden by the three men. It gave him a little added Mexican travel insurance.

He passed the next two hours waiting under a brush arbor that had been put together earlier that morning. The rest was good for his leg. Ortega, who had no medicines, did give him a piece of strong green soap; Slocum washed out the gash, which had clotted nicely by now, and bound a fresh bandage over it. He washed out the old one and dried it in the fierce sun, preparing to use it later in the day.

At the end of the two hours Ortega came for him. He simply beckoned Slocum with a crooked forefinger. Slocum rose and left the shade of the arbor, limping painfully, using a broken branch for a cane. The three men were still tied to their same trees. They looked much worse off than before.

"Well?" Ortega demanded impatiently.

"They persist," Arango said. He looked angry and hot.

"Well, then," Ortega said. "Go ahead."

"Do you want to be blindfolded?" Arango asked.

"No. Shoot," one of them said.

"*Ah, que alma tienes!*" Arango said, almost admiringly, "what guts you have!"

He shot each one over the heart. The blow of the heavy lead bullet forced the air out of each man's mouth with a sound like "Hough!" Their bloody heads slumped forward. For a moment Arango stared at them, watching the flies that began to settle on the blood. Then he shrugged and reloaded.

"Bury them," Ortega said, almost indifferently. "We are not savages." He turned to Slocum, "Now we are friends again! You see how we dispense justice in revolutionary Mexico! Bandits must be treated like the lice they are. Especially those in our midst. Do you agree?"

"Very true," Slocum said. He had regained his composure. "To see one's own men, *mi general*, perform such a traitorous act—I understand how furious you must be."

"Yes, yes." Ortega stared keenly at Slocum's face. It was clear to Slocum that the Mexican was not sure whether Slocum was dealing in double meanings with his last remark, or whether the American had meant what he said.

"Oh, I am ashamed!" Ortega went on, satisfied at last that Slocum was serious. He took off his *sombrero* and wiped his face with a filthy bandanna. The heat was pressing on them like a quilt of heavy wool. "It is all my fault. I should not have let you go without an escort. But this time I will remedy the matter."

Slocum did not like the sound of this. "It is not necessary," he said promptly. "Another horse will do. I will be able to handle anything that might happen—especially since I will check out my gun before I start. I can strip my saddle from the chestnut. I have abused your hospitality long enough, *mi general.*"

175

"I shall not hear of it!"

Ortega gave a few sharp orders. Five horses were caught and saddled. Four men were chosen to form the escort. Arango stood whispering in Ortega's ear. Slocum pretended to be pleased as he examined the four men, who stood holding their horses' bridles. Ortega stood bareheaded in the shadow of the arbor, slouching against the crude wooden upright. He talked quietly to Arango, who nodded with a delighted grin and then transmitted Ortega's instructions to the men of the escort. Slocum pretended to be tightening his cinches, but a quick glance showed him that the men of the escort were looking at him with cold, appraising stares. Slocum knew that he would be in a lot of trouble with this particular group of friends. Oh, oh, Slocum thought, grimly, and in some kind of grudging admiration, one would have to get up early to outwit Ortega. He mounted. His guns were loaded. That would be some consolation. On the other hand, even if he were armed and ready, to travel with four armed men, each of whom probably had his orders to destroy him, gave him an uncomfortable feeling, especially when he was a couple of hundred miles into Mexico.

"There!" Ortega said with satisfaction glowing on his face. "Four men. Two ride in front, two in back, No one will dare attack you, *no one* will get through this escort!"

Especially from inside, Slocum thought ironically.

"But there will be too much attention attracted with so large an escort," Slocum said, making one last try. "It would be best for me to travel alone."

"No," Ortega insisted.

And why not, Slocum thought ruefully. The group would attract no attention for the simple reason that they expected to be back before sunrise. This was why none of them was taking the usual ration of *pinole*. Here was where Ortega slipped up in his protestations of

176

an escort for the ride to the border: two days. And return? Another two. Why didn't any of the escort carry four days' ration? It was very obvious, but Ortega was so anxious that he had forgotten to insist on that little bit of camouflage. Slocum limped away to the little stream that supplied the water to the camp; he had to renew his bandage once more. The unusual exertion of getting ready and saddling the horse had reopened his cut. He sat under a branch of a cottonwood, completetly hidden in its shade, and while he soaked and rinsed out the bandage, two of the escort drifted down for one last drink of water. They lay flat on their bellies 15 feet up the stream. Slocum heard them very clearly, as their low-pitched voices carried over the water.

"Why not take all his money?" one said.

"Did you see what happened to the others?" the other retorted. "*Hombre,* you must be crazy! Besides, we do nothing until he picks up his paper money, those are the orders."

"I know that, you fool. I mean, when he does that, why do we have to ride back to Ortega? Mexico is very big, *amigo.*"

"Yes. But Arango knows where my mother lives."

"What a pity." They were silent a while.

"The *gringo* is very smart. He said they had taken all his money."

"Yes. We must be very careful with him. When he gets the paper money, we kill him fast, *fast*! We do not listen to him talk, understood?"

"Yes, all right. Fill your canteen. Arango will be nervous by now."

Slocum waited till their footsteps had died away, thinking. So. Ortega had decided that when the men said they had not taken the paper money as well as the gold, they were telling the truth. So Slocum knew he was perfectly safe as long as the paper money was not in his

177

possession. Once he had it, he was dead. There was no way he could handle four armed men ready to kill him. He gave the men plenty of time to get back. He then proceeded to make a wide detour and came back into the camp from another direction. He was sure that no one would think he had overheard them.

He mounted painfully, grimacing with the exertion and the anguish. Ortega had insisted on the *abrazo* first. Slocum had returned it, smiling. He did not want Ortega to have the faintest idea that he was anything but delighted to have this escort. Once in the saddle, Slocum looked down. Ortega was lolling on his blanket, smoking a cigarette. He looked upward with a grin, but Slocum detected something cold and calculating in Ortega's expression. It was evident that Ortega had decided that he could handle gun and ammunition purchases himself, or through a cheaper intermediary. He would much rather put the money in his treasury and then look around for another gun salesman. He must feel that he knows by now how to handle it all by himself, Slocum thought grimly. And it was very possible; this Ortega was a smart Mexican. Ortega's smile showed that he expected to see Slocum again—but as a very dead Slocum. Slocum would bet fifty to one that Ortega had told the escort there would be no assumption on their part that they had killed him. He would like to see Slocum brought back dead across the saddle, face downward, legs tied to the hands by a rawhide strip passed around the horse's belly.

Slocum regretted that he had not killed Arango before leaving, but there were some pleasures that reality simply could not accommodate. But the future, Slocum told himself, was like a mango—it would ripen at its own pace. And the flavor could be delicious.

35

They trotted out of the camp. Slocum's leg was aching, but at least there was no bleeding. Slocum thought that the men were all around him like honeysuckle on a front porch. Two men rode in front of him with machetes in leather scabbards. They could whip them out with the speed of a striking rattler, and the up position of the arm when it reached the machete handle, just before pulling the razor-sharp blade, gave the man a perfect opportunity to strike downward in any direction, without a warning. *Macheteros* must never be underestimated, Slocum knew. The two men in the back carried Mausers. Slocum had his Colt, and he had made sure it was loaded. The four men would be wary of that, of course. They would, no doubt, get him to turn around on some sort of a pretext, and then they would all go for him at once, if the men in the rear would not shoot him in the back. But that would create problems for them, for the men in front would have to be warned first so that they would not be hit by the same bullets that had just gone through Slocum. So they would have to group in some way before there would be an attack on him from the rear. The act of the regrouping, or some sort of an urgent signal passing between the rear and the vanguard, would alert Slocum. There was no other way to handle a skillful, deadly gunfighter, which they knew Slocum to be.

The moon had risen. Now plenty of light was pouring down from the cloudless sky. Three miles out of the camp Slocum noticed, at a little road which crossed their trail, stood a statue of the Virgin of Guadalupe. She was small, only two feet tall, but the two men in front of him crossed themselves in the Mexican manner, with the sign of the cross across their chests, and terminated with a kiss on their right thumbnails. The gesture was repeated by the men in back as soon as they drew abreast of the Virgin. A large tin can had been nailed to the post under her, and it was full of roadside flowers, all shriveled up. It was clear that there had been no recent donations.

Slocum held up his hand. The escort stopped, curious. No one was nervous or tense; Slocum knew it was because they must have been told to wait until he had picked up his saddlebags with the paper money. Then they would kill him as quickly as possible. No doubt Arango would require proof. His severed head? Why not? A good hard blow with a sharp machete could do it. And what finer proof could a reasonable man want?

So they halted, friendly and curious. Slocum rode up to the Virgin. He pulled out the dried flowers and dropped them onto the ground.

"What are you giving her instead? Marijuana?" one of the *macheteros* asked.

"He's not a Catholic," his partner muttered. "If he is going to piss in that can I will kill him right now!"

Slocum opened his *morral*. He pulled it off the saddle horn, tipped it upside down above the tin can, and calmly let the gold coins cascade out till the can was filled to the brim. "It's all yellow," he said. "You can call it piss if you want." The three other men laughed. Slocum pulled the *morral* off, pulled the cord shut, and hung it once more on the horn. He estimated that there was at least a thousand dollars in gold heaped up in the battered rusty can. More than she had ever received in such a wayside shrine, but cheap as an investment if it would save his life.

"Although I'm not a Catholic," Slocum said, observing the sudden tense fascination with which the escort was

180

staring at the can brimming now with its gold, "I know how to reciprocate for the many favors she has done for me." He took off his *sombrero* and bowed to the shrine. "She would probably consider that if I crossed myself it would be in bad taste for a Protestant," he said with the proper reverent air, "but I do not think she will be offended if I remove my hat in her honor. *Vamonos!*"

He replaced his *sombrero* and turned his horse's head to the road again. The escort began to move automatically, and then they stopped. It was clear to Slocum that no one trusted the others. There was more money in the tin can than most of them would ever see at once in their whole lives, and each one of them knew it. Paper money meant very little to these peons; United States paper money had as much lure for them as an old newspaper—but *gold!* With these coins in their pockets, any one of them could go away somewhere, far from Tamaulipas and the revenge of Arango, buy a little farm, marry well, buy a good horse, very good boots, and a handsome Winchester. People would take off their hats and call them *Don*. A man's whole life could be changed instantaneously with the contents from that rusty tin can.

And, moreover, all four peons were in front of him now.

"*Vamonos!*" Slocum repeated sharply. No one moved.

One of the men carrying Mausers said, "*Señor.* Consider: It is appreciated what you have done. The Virgin will remember you. Of that there is no doubt in my mind. But, unfortunately, the *sierra* around here is full of thieves—"

"Like those who attacked me last night?"

"*Sí, señor,*" the man said gravely. "Like those *desgraciados*. Around here there are many liars and anti-Christs. If we leave that money, I assure you that it will be gone an hour after sunrise."

181

"Perhaps," Slocum said. "But, consider also: *that* may be the Virgin's wish."

"I doubt it, *señor*. I urge that the money be given to a church. The priest will carry out her wishes."

"Not the priest *I* know, *maricón!*" shouted one of the *macheteros*. "He screws all of the Indian girls who come to confess; he confesses them in his bed on Sunday mornings; he has at least twelve children. I swear on my mother that this is true!"

"That does not matter, *amigo*. The priest is still better than to leave the money there. Any idiot can see that. Would you not agree, *señor*?"

The affair was going well, Slocum thought, even better than he had hoped for. It was time to throw some more kerosene on the fire.

"I do not know your priest, *hombre*," he said judiciously "Perhaps you are right. But perhaps your friend is right as well."

But his help was not necessary.

Slocum heard, "Are you calling me an idiot?"

The voice was calm and level. The others knew that this was a dangerous moment.

"If you wish to consider yourself an idiot I cannot stop you. But no, *amigo, mío*, I do not consider you an idiot. On the other hand, it *is* true that from the age of nine you have been fucking your mother——"

It was the most terrible and unforgiveable of Mexican insults. The man was not able to finish the sentence. The other man's machete came out and down so quickly that Slocum could only see a shining blur in the air. The blade bit deeply into the junction of the victim's neck and right shoulder with an audible *thunk*! Slocum knew that the blade must have cut through the man's shoulder blade. Blood spouted up into the air from a severed artery. He looked at it in amazement and shouted angrily, "Pablito! Get the son of a whore!"

Pablito was one of the two men with Mausers. Pablito had obviously been worried at the start of the dispute. He was ready. He had placed the Mauser across the saddle just in back of the saddle horn, and when his friend cried out for revenge, he pulled back the Mauser's bolt and worked a cartridge into the chamber. Then he fired. The *machetero* received the heavy slug in his stomach and the impact knocked him out of his saddle. The blast of the explosion, only a few inches from the ears of the rifleman's untrained horse, was too much for the animal. He reared and then fell backwards, pinning his rider under him and at the same time breaking the man's hip.

Slocum stared slack-jawed at the three downed men. Now, suddenly, thanks to the Virgin, there was only one man left, the second *machetero*. That man was staring in amazement at the three men who were down.

"Let us pull the horse off Pablito," Slocum said.

"*Sí, sí!*" the man said. He dismounted and ran toward the fallen horse, which was struggling to get to its feet, causing even more fractures inside the man's already-broken hip. Pablito was screaming in agony. Enough people had suffered that night, Slocum decided, so he reached forward and stunned the fourth man with the butt of his Colt instead of killing him. He dismounted and picked up the two Mausers. One *machetero* would die soon, one rifleman was dead, one had a smashed pelvis and would limp for the rest of his life, and the fourth man was unconscious. Slocum unhooked his *morral*, bent down over the Virgin, and scooped back all the gold coins.

"She helped me, no?" he said softly to the man with the broken hip. He drew the drawstring tight and hooking the *morral* over his horn, rode north, holding on to the two Mausers. When he reached a dense growth of *mesquite*, he flung one of the Mausers into it as far as he could. A few minutes more brought him to his cache. He dismounted painfully, rolled over the protective covering of stones, unearthed the two saddlebags, and slung them across his horse's withers. The weather began to cloud up quickly; in a few minutes it began to rain, steadily and persistently. When he came to a stony patch he cut east across it, heading for Monterrey on the principle that Ortega would think he would be heading straight for the States by the most direct route. The rain would wipe out his tracks, and with luck he would be able to board a train at Monterrey for Laredo or Brownsville. That is, if Ortega somehow didn't find out, through questioning various peons, whether or not they might have seen a *gringo* riding north, heading for the Rio Grande.

He rode all night, pressing hard with his left palm across his thigh to somehow ease the pain. At sunrise, weary and sleepy beyond belief, he finally rode into Monterrey.

36

He was still wearing the clothes that he had been attacked in. He had buttoned up his jacket against the cold rain. That served, of course, to hide the fact that he was not wearing a shirt. His pants had a slash where the machete had bitten into his leg, and there were still some bloodstains around the tear. Rain dropped off his *sombrero*. He could look like a hard-bitten cowpuncher with plenty of signs of wear on his equipment, so he did not attract much attention. Nevertheless, it would be a good idea to attract even less. He found a second-hand clothing store. He outfitted himself quickly in clean but

184

well-worn American rancher's clothing. The town, being so close to the border, was full of American products. As he changed into the clothes in the back of the store, he removed the bandage from his leg. The cut was inflamed and purplish. Bad; he would have to see a doctor, and that meant one person more who would know about an American wounded in the right leg—if Ortega came to Monterrey he'd be asking around for a *gringo* who limped. Slocum had bought an extra shirt. He would be seeing a doctor in Texas; right now he dared not visit a druggist to buy bandages. He tore up the extra shirt and bandaged his leg.

Next he found a livery stable. It was owned by an amiable ex-cowpuncher named Santiago Ramirez. Slocum dismounted and asked Ramirez if he wanted to buy the horse. Ramirez walked out, munching a *tortilla*, walked once around the horse, looked inside its mouth and made him a fair offer. Slocum accepted it immediately. He did not want to walk around Monterrey buying a ticket, or food, with his gold *pesos* or his American money. Both were things which people would remember too well.

Don Santiago knew the timetable for the trains running to the border. The next train for Texas, he said, would be leaving at 8:47. He said it left on time because the train was infected by the spirit of punctuality, being so close to the border. He had two hours to kill, Slocum thought and smiled to himself at the phrase.

"Are you hungry, *señor*?"

Slocum admitted hunger. "Where is there a restaurant?"

"I cannot permit this," he said. "They are no good. Please accept my poor hospitality. It would be an honor. And if you wish, I will send my boy to buy your ticket for you. You look very tired." Slocum accepted the offer.

185

The boy was 11, alert and intelligent. His name was Gustavo, but because he was overweight, his father affectionately called him "Gordito," the little fat one. Gordito made extra money by selling the violently colored Mexican candies from a little tray, and his sideline was boot-polishing. He ran off cheerfully with Slocum's money to the ticket office while Slocum sat down to eat.

Señora Ramirez brought out eggs and *tortillas* and fresh tomatoes. Slocum ate hungrily. *Don* Santiago talked. He had managed, by a miracle, he admitted, to save enough money to buy the stable from an uncle. Now it gave him a good living and his rheumatism did not trouble him so much. He was very curious about an American being in Mexico—an American who spoke such good Spanish!

Slocum knew that the man's interest had to be soothed. "I was a foreman on a *hacienda*," he began. "Near Saltillo. It was owned by an American. He asked me to come down and work there because I spoke Spanish."

"You speak it well, *señor*."

"*Gracias.* But he and I got along badly. I quit. We fought——"

"Did you kill him, *señor*?"

"No. We fought American style, with our fists. I won, but he would not pay me. So I took one of his horses—and left. I hope this will not inconvenience you."

"No," said *Don* Santiago. He laughed. "It is a fine horse, and I will sell him quickly. There will be no problems."

"Well, then," finished Slocum, "having no money, wanting to return to Texas, needing good clothes, and a ticket on the railroad—I sold him to you. The saddle I want, it is a good one."

"Yes. It is too far to walk to the station, *señor*. With your permission, I will drive you."

Don Santiago hitched up a buggy. Only by using grim determination was Slocum able to walk to it without limping. If Ortega did come to Monterrey, he would be searching for a limping *gringo*. He tossed the saddle into the buggy without wincing. He casually tossed the saddle-bags on top of the saddle, as if they contained nothing more than some extra socks and some shaving equipment. He had slung his *morral* over one shoulder, and had inserted a box of revolver shells in it, which would explain its weight if anyone were to glance at it casually. Into the top he had carelessly jammed two brand-new bandannas; and their brilliant crimson color advertised to anyone who happened to notice that the *morral* held nothing important, just a few odds and ends that any traveling cowpuncher might have picked up in town after a hard season on the range. He looked exactly like what he was trying to look like: an experienced *gringo* ranch foreman journeying with his saddle; a man who had just quit his job and was looking elsewhere for a new position.

The buggy moved slowly through the streets of Monterrey. Slocum slid down in his seat as much as possible, pretending to sleep. His *sombrero* was tilted over his eyes. But an American cowpuncher in a buggy with his saddle beside him was not an ordinary sight anywhere, and many people, amused to see a saddle occupying a buggy seat, paused to smile. Slocum did not like this at all. Besides, his leg was throbbing. The more he thought about it, the more enraged he became. He would like to reciprocate, and the thought of meeting Ortega or Arango became more and more appealing.

Don Santiago wanted to talk. He was bored, and he liked to chat with strangers whom he considered educated. He himself could not read, and he respected anyone who could. He asked questions continuously; he was thus making up for his lost education.

But this morning he insisted on imparting information. "We have had a very big kidnapping," he said importantly. "Have you heard?"

"No, *Don* Santiago."

"Many bandits seized a rich man from Torreón, a very rich man. They cut him many times, nothing fatal, until he agreed to give them 3,000,000 *pesos*. So people say. But, *señor*, I would be embarrassed to ask the people I know how much a million is. Because they would laugh at me and call me an ignorant *burro* behind my back. But, *señor*, I see that you are an intelligent person and that you have gone to school. Is this true?"

"It is true, *señor*."

"*Bueno*! And you will be leaving Monterrey on the 8:47 and will not return?"

"That is likely."

"Then *señor*, since I will not see you again, please tell me how much a million is."

"Well," said Slocum, "let me see, let me see. . . ." He mused. "Yes! You see the cobblestones in the street?"

"*Sí, señor.*"

Slocum knew that Don Santiago could count, even though he could not read.

"How many are there, if you were to walk in a straight line from one side of the street to the other?"

Don Santiago reined his horse. After a minute he turned to Slocum and announced proudly, "Thirty-five."

"Now, how long would it take you to walk from one side of the street to the other? Not running, just walking?"

"Ten seconds, maybe."

"Now, imagine that I have taken one million cobblestones. I have laid them in a straight line. Suppose you were to begin walking along them, at your normal pace, without stopping, day and night——"

"*Sí, sí!* I understand. *Without* stopping!"

"Yes. Let me see." Slocum worked it out in his head. It would take 79 hours. "*Don* Santiago," he said, "you would start walking on Monday morning at sunrise, say at six. You will arrive at the end of the millionth cobblestone at lunch on Thursday."

"*Thursday?*"

"*Sí, señor.*"

"What a miracle is the human mind! How far is it above animals, even my dog Benjamin, who is very smart! I am forever in your debt, *señor!* Monday at sunrise to lunch on Thursday! How clear! How easy to comprehend! I am sure not a single businessman in Monterrey could have answered me with such clarity and such intelligence!"

"You flatter me too much, *Don* Santiago." Slocum was touched by the lavish but obviously sincere praise. The mental arithmetic had taken Slocum's mind off his leg, but now it was beginning to hurt again.

"You are in pain, *señor.*"

His denial would not be believed, Slocum knew.

"Somewhat," he said reluctantly.

"We are close to a doctor."

"I would prefer to avoid him."

"Ah." *Don* Santiago stared ahead.

The *gringo* had come in with a horse which was not his. He had probably been wounded during the theft of the horse. But it was a good horse and he would make a good profit when he would sell it. And the *gringo* had told him how much a million was without laughing at him. He deserved a favor.

"He is a very discreet doctor, *señor.* Trust me."

Slocum knew there were times when he had to trust his instincts. Moreover, he did not want to arrive in Texas with gangrene, and there was an angry reddish

189

tinge to the wound he did not like. And in gangrene, hours counted.

"All right," he said.

The buggy turned into a narrow street and halted. *Don* Santiago jumped down and pounded on a huge brass knocker set into an oak door reinforced with iron straps. It opened. He whispered. The door swung open.

"This way, *señor*. I will watch your saddle and saddle-bags." Slocum decided to trust him. He clambered down painfully; the leg was getting worse by the minute. *Don* Santiago whispered, "The doctor does mostly abortions for unfortunate girls. He takes care of the whores, you see. But he is a very good doctor."

He was. He looked at the badly swollen thigh. He shook his head. He opened the gash, probed, cleaned it thoroughly, while Slocum clenched his hands to prevent moaning. The doctor held up a few dirty threads of fabric which the machete stroke had forced into the cut. From behind the threads suddenly oozed pus. Slocum felt relief immediately. The doctor swabbed it inside and out thoroughly with carbolic acid. "In a few more hours you would have had gangrene, *señor*. You are lucky, indeed." He stitched the gash neatly and placed a clean dressing on it. "Be sure to see another doctor tomorrow. You will be where you can see a doctor?"

"Yes, doctor. I will be in Tampico."

"Fine, fine. There are plenty of good doctors there."

Slocum put on his pants. He fished a gold coin out of his pocket.

"More than enough, *señor*," said the doctor.

"Then treat someone for nothing."

"*Como no? Adiós, señor.*"

The first person he saw as he stepped out of the room was the whore he had chosen at the brothel. Sitting beside her was the madam. The girl was very nervous

190

and the madam was patting her soothingly on the shoulder. The girl did not look up as he went by, but the madam did, and she stared involuntarily as she saw his face. It was obvious to Slocum that she had recognized him. No one but she saw Slocum's next gesture: He raised his thumb and forefinger as if he held a gun, pointed the forefinger at her and smiled. She paled but nodded. Slocum went out through the door. He hoped that she would take the threat seriously: Madams everywhere were confirmed realists.

He got into the buggy. His leg was feeling much better. If she got into conversation with the doctor about him— and she might, since they obviously knew each other— she would find out that he intended to leave for Tampico tomorrow. Tomorrow, then, if she talked to various officials, the *rurales* would be watching the station.

Don Santiago carried his saddle inside the station for him, while Slocum negligently carried his saddlebags. They attracted hardly any attention at all, as Slocum had hoped; plenty of Americans came and went out of Monterrey on business, and so common was the sight that they attracted none of the attention they would have drawn had they been, for instance, in Torreón. *Don* Santiago set down the saddle. Slocum reached into his pocket for a coin.

"*Ah no, amigó mío!* It is my great pleasure. But one question. How long would it take me to walk along *three* million cobblestones?"

Slocum thought for a few seconds. Then he said, "Nine full days and twenty-one hours."

"*Señor*, I will *never* be able to repay you for telling me what a million is. *Buen viaje!*"

They shook hands. *Don* Santiago drove off. Slocum sat down on the platform with his back against the saddle. He sat on the saddlebags. There was no way anyone could attempt to slide them from underneath him. A window back of his head opened into the waiting room. He had half an hour wait for his train. There was another leaving at 8:01 for the south. He was informed of this by a sloppily printed timetable which had been glued to the station wall. The station and the platform began filling up with Indians returning to their isolated villages with their unsold pots, harnesses, *reatas*, chickens, tomatoes, whips, and pigs. Turkeys, tied with string around their ankles, squawked and fluttered indignantly. They had begun to flow into the station minutes after Slocum had sat down, and, as Indians always did in the presence of *mestizos* and Spaniards, they maintained silence. Slocum was surrounded by the mass of black-haired Indians; the group extended to the edge of the platform. He sat against his saddle, amused at the serious, grave faces of the tiny Indian babies.

It was hot and the press of people made it worse. He took off his jacket and *sombrero*. Now, with his black hair and his white shirt, and with his height camouflaged by his slouching backwards against the saddle, and with his tanned face, he blended into the Indian crowd. He pretended to be asleep. After a few minutes they paid him no attention, and, convinced that he was asleep, he watched the fathers, through his half-closed eyes, affectionately dandle and tickle their babies.

Through the window behind him he heard a well-known voice speak in crisp, commanding tones to the ticket agent. He did not turn his head. The voice was that of Colonel Escalante. He was saying, "There are three men I am looking for. If you see them, send for me immediately, at the Presidio. You will be well taken care of."

"Understood, *mi coronel*."

"Listen carefully. One is about five-ten. He is dark, black straight hair, big shoulders. He looks like a *mestizo*.

192

Part Yaqui. He speaks very good Spanish. He has black eyes. He is forty. The second man is much shorter; he is about thirty. He has brown eyes and two scars on the back of his left hand. *Mestizo*. This one never smiles. His Spanish is not very good. Then there is the third. He is a *gringo*. A little over six feet. Wide shoulders, green eyes, black hair, speaks Spanish like a Mexican."

"Understood."

"Very good." Slocum turned his head slightly. Through his half-closed eyes, submerged still in a sea of black heads, Slocum watched Escalante stride arrogantly through the station, as his two aides rudely pushed Indians out of the way. A man like Escalante, Slocum thought gratefully, never looked at Indians; they were literally beneath his notice. Thus, the safest place for Slocum to be would be right where he was. And with satisfaction, Slocum observed that the colonel looked exhausted. He must have been doing a lot of hard patrolling lately over the surrounding countryside. And with no luck whatsoever—thank God, as far as Slocum was concerned. But when it came to the two Mexicans, Slocum heartily wished him all the luck in the world. But with all that ransom money still in Ortega's hands, it didn't seem as if Escalante would get anywhere near them. Still, one could never predict anything in Mexico with any degree of accuracy. It was one of the charms of the place for Slocum. Now he noticed, through the door of the station, the cafe opposite; two *rurales* were sitting at a sidewalk table, each with a Mauser between his legs. They were obviously posted there to carry on with Escalante's search. Slocum seriously hoped that Ortega would not show up at the last minute. A lot of excitement would be generated that would hamper his discreet departure. He saw Escalante giving instructions to the two *rurales*, who had leaped to their feet at his approach. Then they saluted. He lifted a finger negligently in

193

response, and as he turned to go, was hailed by Aurelio Gutierrez.

This was interesting to Slocum. Why should the man be in town? Surely there was nothing he could do of any value in the search for and apprehension of his kidnappers. Then why was he here? It was a puzzle. His purpose would probably bear investigating. But how?

Gordito came by, his shoeshine box slung over his shoulder, holding his tray of candies. As he passed among the crowd on the platform, Slocum beckoned him over. The boy weaved his way in and out of the Indians and came to a halt in front of him. Slocum picked out a few red and a few green candies, liberally sprinkled with coconut. No one bothered to look at him except some of the Indian children. As he made his selection, Slocum spoke quietly. "Across the street is a café. A colonel is talking there to a fat man. I want to know everything they talk about." The boy nodded. Slocum paid him for the candies and Gordito left.

To any casual observer, the whole transaction would seem perfectly natural. Slocum gave the candies away to the nearest children while their mothers smiled their thanks. Slocum nodded at them and watched Gordito make his way across the street. He promptly kneeled at Escalante's feet, and in the efficient way of Mexican bootblacks, simply took Escalante's right boot and placed it on his box. Escalante was startled, and looking down, saw it was a bootblack. He placed a hand on the boy's shoulder and shoved hard. The boy tumbled into the gutter. Gutierrez looked distressed and spoke sharply to Escalante, and when Gordito assembled his box and rearranged his spilled candies, invited the boy to polish *his* shoes. Slocum smiled; he had no idea that Gutierrez possessed any quality of even this minimal compassion. Good for him.

Gordito began his cleaning, application of polish, and then a long, careful polishing job. He spent ten minutes on it. The shoes were so brilliant that they reflected the sun, as even Slocum could observe across the street. Gutierrez looked down absentmindedly, patted Gordito on the head, and gave him a coin. The two men walked up the street, leaving the *rurales* restlessly watching everyone who walked by.

Gordito made his way back to Slocum. Once more Slocum pretended to be making a careful selection of candies, while the boy spoke quickly and clearly. "The fat man said that all the time he was walking back at night from the railroad he was thinking. He was thinking that if there should actually be a phos—a phos—a——"

"Phosphoferrite?"

"Yes, *señor*. That word. A mine with that in it. If there should be such a mine near Monterrey, it would be perfect. The location, the railroad, how close it was to the United States, water, wood. So as soon as he got into town, he telegraphed someone in Torreón, someone with an English name—"

"Burton?"

"*Sí, señor!* He wanted him to look around here, to prospect. It was crazy, he said, but why not? And this *Señor* Burton came next day and talked to some American mining engineers in Monterrey. He found a man who had located an outcrop of this material, but since the man was only interested in gold or silver, he didn't think much about it. So *Señor* Burton gave him a couple of thousand *pesos*, and this man showed it to *Señor* Burton, and it was only ten miles away. He thinks there is a great deal of it underground. So he is going to put the Englishman in charge of the mine, and in charge of building a factory. Then the two men laughed very hard, and the fat one gave me a *peso*, and they went away, *señor*."

Well, thought Slocum, half-amused, half-bitter. That's life. I imagined something which actually exists! It will make him a millionaire many times over, and it cost him, after all, only a couple hundred thousand *pesos*. That's very little. In a sense, he went on, some of the profit from that future match factory was *his*. It would be interesting to come down this way again in a couple of years and collect some royalties from Gutierrez. Still, if Ghislaine would still be with him, the factory would be a big help in paying for her pearl necklaces and her frequent trips to Paris. I could collect some of those match profits and then meet her in Paris. Life was hilarious, Slocum thought. He reached into his *morral* and gave Gordito a 20-*peso* gold coin.

"*Señor!*" the boy protested. "This is too much."

"The information is worth it, *chico. Muchas gracias.*"

"I must go now and clean out the stable, *señor. Muchas gracias. Adiós, señor.*"

"*Adiós.*" Slocum distributed the candy he had bought this time and then dozed off, unable to keep his eyes open anymore.

37

Someone was shaking his shoulder violently. His hand went automatically to his Colt butt, but he recognized *Don* Santiago's voice.

"*Señor!* I rode here quickly!"

Immediately afterwards Slocum heard the train whistle as it approached its first grade crossing in Monterrey.

"*Que pasa, hombre?*" The Indians had gone.

"Two men rode into my stable a little while ago. They

recognized your horse. They asked my boy where the *gringo* was who owned the horse. He said he did not know. They started to beat him. I was not there. I was walking the buggy horse to cool her off; they did not see me. They are wearing guns and they have Mausers, too. I jumped on the buggy horse and rode her here bareback. They will probably come here next. Why else would you sell me your horse, except to take the train back to the United States?"

They would walk right into the trap of the *rurales!* Excellent, Slocum thought. He sat back and smiled. "Do not worry, *Don* Santiago," he said, "your boy will be avenged."

"How?" the man demanded. His face was flushed with rage. "I have no gun! What shall I do? I don't even have a machete!"

"Be patient, *amigo mío*. There are people close who are waiting for those two men to come here. You will see. If you see the two men, do not move, you will be caught in the cross fire."

"Who will shoot them?"

"The two *rurales* across the street."

"There are no *rurales, señor*."

Slocum looked. *Don* Santiago was right. The café table was empty. Slocum stood and looked up and down the street. They were nowhere in sight. The sons of whores, Slocum swore bitterly to himself. They have gone off to another *pulquería* or to a whorehouse! This changed everything. He stood up and checked his Colt. There would be no slipup this time. He slung the saddlebags over one shoulder and the *morral* over the other. The train whistle came closer.

"Now, listen carefully, *Don* Santiago. I'm leaving the saddle right here. When they come in they will think I'm still in town somewhere, that I've missed this train, that

197

maybe I stepped into a whorehouse and forgot about the train. Because it's too good a saddle to leave behind. I'm going to take this train. When they finally give up and leave the station, I want you to keep the saddle. It's yours. Do you understand?"

Don Santiago nodded. "Don't worry," Slocum said, "these men do not make war on children."

Ramírez stared at him with some contempt. Slocum had thought many things very quickly: that he could stay here and fight it out with Ortega and Arango. But, in that case, if he were to win, the train would have come and gone—and the shooting would attract the attention of the *rurales* from whatever brothel or *pulquería* they had disappeared into. And if they came, Escalante would come. And that would be the end. No, better to go now and accept Ramírez's contempt.

The locomotive rounded a curve. Slocum decided it would be best to get on the train from the other side. He did not offer to shake hands. He knew *Don* Santiago would refuse. Slocum walked across the platform, stepped down onto the roadbed, thence across the tracks to the far side. The train came puffing and clanging into the station and hissed finally to a stop. Steam jetted from the stack and from crevices all over the boiler area. It was not very well maintained, but it moved, and that was all that Slocum wanted: something that would move to the north and take him in a few hours safely into the United States and away from this country where people killed each other as casually as flies.

Now he was completely shielded from any view from the station area. He swung up the steps and waited a moment; several people were jammed in the vestibule as they prepared to descend to the platform on the other side. The last passenger to dismount was an old lady in a black dress. She carried a hatbox and a rolled-up black silk umbrella which she was preparing to open up as a sunshade. There were no porters to help her. She had a heavy, buckled valise and she turned and looked up at Slocum appealingly. It was obviously too much for her to handle by herself; no doubt a son had put her on the train and had carried everything on for her.

Slocum knew it would be too risky for him to help her. Ortega moved too fast and unexpectedly for him to take that chance. He shrugged his shoulders with a helpless little smile. She glared up at him, and then, panting with exertion, reached up to grab the handle of her heavy valise. A brown hand slid up over hers and closed round the handle. In the center of the back of the hand were two parallel scars. Slocum froze; he did not move for his gun less the movement itself attract attention.

Arango turned with the valise in his scarred hand and walked beside the old lady, who was busily complaining about the poor manners of the disgusting young man on the train who had refused to help her. Slocum could see them both now, Arango taking long steps across the platform as he headed for the door opening into the station, and the old lady trotting beside him, looking up into his face, and talking a blue streak. Arango reached out his other hand and took her hatbox. He would not have thought that Arango had such consideration for anyone, but perhaps, thought Slocum ironically, Arango did not regard old ladies as his natural prey. It was not much fun to shoot them.

Slocum moved deeper into the vestibule. From that angle he could just make out Arango's squat, broad body walking slowly, to keep pace with the old lady's short steps, and he could also see her excited gestures and then another indignant glare back in Slocum's direction. He was being denounced. But it was clear, from the way that Arango was swinging his head left and right, that he was not listening to the old lady's recital of her grievances. He was looking for any signs of Slocum. Beyond the two figures was the door into the station itself. In the dim light of the interior, Slocum could see his saddle, with *Don* Santiago standing beside it and talking to someone.

Arango and the old lady entered the station. The train jerked and slowly began to move. Slocum let out a long sigh of relief, and the tension began to drain out of him.

Arango suddenly moved faster. He dropped the suitcase and hatbox, paying no attention to the angry expostulations of the old lady. He now stood facing *Don* Santiago. The window opening into the station was so large that Slocum could see everything, even though the train was moving. Then the three figures shifted their positions. *Don* Santiago was retreating, and now Ortega came into view. He had a young boy next to him and Slocum saw that it was Gordito. He could see the glint of a gun barrel. The boy's face was badly bruised, in long red welts, which, Slocum saw, must have been made by the gun barrel. The muzzle of the gun was dug into the boy's neck. *Don* Santiago's face was an angry, flushed red.

They must have been trying to find out where he was, Slocum thought. If the saddle was there, he was obviously coming back. Slocum could imagine the questions. Did he go to some café? Was he buying something to take back? Was he in a brothel? Which one? Was he drunk? They had beaten the boy badly, it looked like, and he must have told them that his father had gone off to see the *gringo*. Now they were forcing *Don* Santiago to tell them where the *gringo* was staying. And was he going to take the next train south? Or had he missed this one to the north?

Arango took the gun from the boy's neck. It had made a red circle in the flesh that Slocum could see even at this distance. Arango lifted the gun barrel and smashed *Don* Santiago in the face. It was a hard, merciless blow, and

Slocum winced. *Don* Santiago spat out three of his front teeth and said nothing. Blood dribbled down his chin. He did not talk. Not more than six seconds had elapsed from the time when Arango had dropped the old lady's valise and hatbox until *Don* Santiago's mouth was smashed. Now the train took Slocum out of sight of the waiting room. Ortega and Arango were not paying any attention to the train, now beginning to pick up speed. It was clear that they were sure that Slocum was still somewhere in Monterrey. Slocum hesitated. He had so much to lose and nothing to gain if he were to intercede now.

Nothing except honor.

38

Once more he saw the flash of the gun barrel going up; then it came slashing down viciously.

That was enough. He felt that old uncontrollable rage bursting its boundaries. He had been able to keep it in check all the time he was in Mexico; he had held it back all the time he had sat hating Arango and not being able to do anything about it. The last sadistic blow of Arango's gun tore down the dam against Slocum's reluctance to become involved.

Slocum threw the saddlebags over his left shoulder and grabbed the *morral* by its drawstring in his left hand. He jumped lightly from the train and landed running. He ran quickly to the platform along one of the iron rails, balancing himself lightly without effort. He didn't want Arango to know of his approach, as the man had a keen sense of hearing and would surely hear had Slocum run along the loose gravel. When he reached the platform area, Slocum still kept running along the rail, so Arango would not hear his footsteps pound on the wood.

When he was still 20 feet from the platform entrance into the station, he heard the boy sobbing. He leaped lightly onto the platform and looked into the window with his Colt ready. Three Indians, who were sitting cross-legged near the window, scrambled frantically to one side as they saw the gun appear in Slocum's hand. Once more he saw Arango lift his gun. No longer could the old lady whom Arango had helped into the station watch this merciless beating. She screamed. It was a shrill, ear-piercing noise, and it angered Arango. For him it was too much to put up with, especially from someone whom he had helped. He turned away from *Don* Santiago and took a step toward her. All of the violent events that immediately followed, as Slocum reconstructed them later, took place within a time span of ten seconds.

As Arango turned toward the old lady, Ortega twisted the boy's arm backwards and up so cruelly that the boy gasped in agony and fell to his knees. The boy was facing Arango in his kneeling position, his face wet with tears. Slocum held fire; he might hit the old lady or the boy. He waited for a clean shot which would not continue on and hit the huddled mass of people who were standing in back of Arango and Ortega in horrified paralysis.

Arango's step toward the screaming woman was taken too hastily. He tripped over Slocum's saddle and as he crashed heavily to the floor, his Colt went flying from his hand. It skidded across the floor and came to a halt against the boy's outstretched right hand. Gordito picked it up. Arango had now come up slightly from his prone, sprawled-out position. He was braced on his knees, preparing to stand up.

"Give it to me," he said softly, but with venomous intensity. "Give it to me, *muchacho*." Ortega twisted the boy's other arm some more. The agony forced him lower, but he brought up the gun's muzzle. He was not strong enough to lift and aim the heavy Colt with any accuracy. The muzzle tumbled and trembled in wild, erratic arcs.

"Give it to me. Or you will wish you had never been born. Now. Give it to me *now*." There was such hatred in his voice that Slocum shook his head in disgust; he knew—and so did the boy—that Arango meant every word he had said. Still on his knees, Arango moved closer. He moved slowly, as if he knew that any sudden move on his part would cause Gordito to fire. He was now only three feet from the muzzle of his own gun. The boy was clearly terrified. His face was white and sweaty wherever there were no welt marks from the earlier blows with the gun barrel. The men's attention was riveted on the boy. Even Ortega was afraid to shoot; it was obvious to Slocum that the general feared that his shot would cause the boy to fire automatically, even if he should be hit. And Ortega was in no way a marksman of the caliber of Arango.

Don Santiago was sprawled at Ortega's feet with both his hands pressed over his bleeding mouth. He sat erect, but the general was so fascinated with Arango's slow crawl toward Gordito and the boy's hypnotized stare that he did not notice. It was like a rattlesnake and a rabbit. Suddenly Ortega felt his gun being withdrawn from its holster. He let the boy's arm go and turned hastily to face this new threat from Ramírez.

Now the boy had both hands free. He brought up the Colt with two trembling hands. Arango's face was now two feet from the muzzle.

Just as Slocum was on the verge of yelling "Arango!" —which would cause the man to turn and thus give him a clear target—Gordito pulled the trigger.

39

The .45 blast bellowed in the old wooden building. The heavy slug, fired from that distance of two feet, hit Arango in his mouth. It smashed his teeth and continued through his mouth, thence through his throat. It continued on and then buried itself in the wall below Slocum's position at the window. Immediately afterward, *Don* Santiago fired. It hit Ortega low in his right side, and then it ranged upwards, smashing through his liver and spleen, cutting through his stomach, and came to a halt inside the rib cage, having gouged along the outside of Ortega's heart for a finale.

Ortega fell on his back, his face twisted in agony, with his right hand pressed against his side. He lay there panting.

Arango was paralyzed from the neck down. He lay prone, the blood from his throat pouring through the smashed, jagged stumps of his teeth. He turned his head and glared up at the boy, who was transfixed with horror as he stared at the dying, paralyzed man who lay choking to death on his own blood.

The old lady had stopped screaming. She had sunk to the floor and was rocking back and forth, whimpering. People were running up. They were coming in from the street. In the distance, Slocum saw the tall sugar-loaf hats of the *rurales*, who were finally showing up. Slocum holstered his gun and moved to one side of the window so that he would not be noticed by the *rurales*.

Arango's eyes were focused on the boy. The glittering, hard quality was still there; Slocum had seen such eyes when he had once found a rattler coiled in his blankets. He had broken its spine with a branch. The snake had turned its head, and unable to move, looked upwards at

Slocum for several seconds. It seemed to Slocum that its eyes were made of concentrated acid.

Slocum knew what Arango was thinking: "I killed many men, many *rurales*, many soldiers. I have fought in many battles, and I have won many battles. I have stolen trains, I have ravaged great *haciendas* and here I am dying on the dirty floor of a railroad station, killed by an 11-year-old *boy!*" He choked and died.

Ortega was panting in agony. He was gritting his teeth to control himself. He looked up at *Don* Santiago and then at the boy, as if to say, "So far I have come, and then to die like this!" He shuddered and died.

People were clustering around the two dead men. The ticket agent bent down and looked at the corpses. Then he began talking excitedly to the two *rurales* and waving his hands. One of them opened his eyes in a wide stare of astonishment, and left. Going to get Escalante, Slocum knew.

The train for Tampico was entering the yards. As it slowly approached, its bell clanging, Slocum decided to get on. It would not be safe to hang around Monterrey, waiting for the next train to the north. He could always get a ship at Tampico for New Orleans. And there was always some sort of action possible in New Orleans. Gunrunning was a popular sport there. As the train slowed, Slocum stepped quickly across the platform and boarded it. After all, he had tripled his investment—and outside of paying some painful brokerage fees, 300 percent profit in Mexico was something a man could be proud of. But no more gunrunning to Mexico. To the border, yes. But, *not an inch inside*. And payment on receipt, no credit.

The train began moving. There was a tense 30 seconds as it moved slowly, but no one came out running. He was safe this time. He went inside the car and settled down in a chair. Monterrey went by, slowly at first, then faster and faster. Cactus, *burros*, flat roofs, girls with lovely long black hair.

Ortega had once told him, *"Como México, no hay dos."*

Literal translation: *Like Mexico, there are not two.* Translate it any way you want, thought Slocum, he was very, very lucky to extract his ass from there in one piece.

GREAT YARNS FROM
ONE OF THE FASTEST-SELLING
WESTERN WRITERS TODAY

JAKE LOGAN